George Melville Baker

The Flowing Bowl

A drama in three acts

George Melville Baker

The Flowing Bowl
A drama in three acts

ISBN/EAN: 9783337343811

Printed in Europe, USA, Canada, Australia, Japan

Cover: Foto ©Andreas Hilbeck / pixelio.de

More available books at **www.hansebooks.com**

A Drama in Three Acts

BY

GEORGE M. BAKER

BOSTON
GEORGE M. BAKER AND COMPANY
No. 10 MILK STREET
1885

CHARACTERS.

MARTIN MOORE, A Slave of the Cup.
MAJOR FITZPATRICK, His Boon Companion.
HERBERT POOLE, Rich and Reckless.
CLIFTON JEROME, A young Lawyer
CHARLIE WILKINS, A too willing Captive.
RICHARD BELL, A Boatman.
PETE, A Black Boy, aged 60
MARION MOORE, The Daughter of ——?
MRS. MORRIS, Martin's Sister.
JESSIE MORRIS, "A Terrible Torment."

COSTUMES.

Martin. — Gray wig, smooth red face, lines strongly marked (but avoid a repulsive red nose); dress suitable for a man of sixty at a summer resort.

Major. — Close-crop reddish wig, and flowing side-whiskers turning gray; red face (careful of the nose); make-up fat. On first appearance, a red handkerchief tied about his head, a long linen duster. On his second appearance, a neat suit of summer wear, duster and handkerchief removed, and a brisk, hearty manner

Poole and Jerome — Handsome summer suits.

Charlie Wilkins. — Yachtsman's suit As the cowboy, pants tucked in boots, red shirt, belt about waist in which are stuck two carving-knives and a pistol, a lasso coiled hung at his belt on the right side, wig of long red hair, long red mustache, and long chin-beard; very broad brim slouch hat.

Richard. — Sailor trousers, shirt, and jacket of blue; black kerchief for neck, straw hat, grizzled wig and beard.

Pete. — Gray wig, mustache, and chin-beard; black suit, white tie; carries himself like a ramrod, with occasional collapses and recoverings, with groans to show that it is hard work

Ladies. — As suit their tastes, their ages, and the place.

THE FLOWING BOWL.

A DRAMA IN THREE ACTS.

ACT I. — *Parlor in a seaside hotel.* C., *in flat, doors open on piazza; set railing to piazza, backed by light-blue curtain to represent sky; long windows* R. *and* L. *in flat, with lace curtains looped* R. *and* L., *pots of flowers or vines in one or both windows; doors* R. *and* L. 2 E.; *lounge* L. *between* 1 *and* 2 E.; *arm-chair* R. *between* 1 *and* 2 E.; *table* C., *opposite doors; arm-chairs* R. *and* L. *of it.* MARION *discovered seated* L. *of table, reading a newspaper;* MRS. MORRIS *on lounge, crocheting.*

MRS. M. Any news, Marion?

MARION. No, auntie, nothing that will interest you, unless it is that old advertisement which re-appears. (*Reads.*) "Five hundred dollars reward for any reliable information concerning Nathan Roberts, a returned Californian who with his daughter landed in New York, Feb. 6, 1865. Address Perkins & Jerome, counsellors at law, New York."

MRS. M. It's the same old story, with a slight change this time. Mr. Perkins has given the missing man a daughter, never mentioned before, and taken to himself a partner. Jerome, Jerome: it can't be —

MARION. Yes, it is, auntie, — our friend Clifton Jerome, whose ears you boxed so unmercifully because he fairly beat you at cards.

MRS. M. He deserved it: he cheated.

MARION. Don't say that, auntie. He is an honorable gentleman: I am glad he has obtained so fine a position. Mr. Perkins has long stood among the leaders in his pro-

5

fession ; and with such an adviser Clifton Jerome, talented, enthusiastic, and determined, has a glorious career before him.

MRS. M.   Ah ! the junior partner is a lucky man.   The eloquence of his appeal to a jury must work wonders, when the mere mention of his name has such an effect upon so cool and so apathetic a nature as yours, Marion.   We must have him down here.

MARION.   Not for the world ! our social circle could have no charms for him.

MRS. M.   Well, I don't know about that.   Here we are comfortably settled in a snug little seaside hotel, with the genial Major Fitzpatrick and the elegant Mr. Poole slaves at our call, and, last but not least, your father, a little grumpy and grouty perhaps as a companion, but a capital manager of the financial department, who sees that we want for nothing money can supply.   You've only to make up your mind to be gay and happy, and the summer will pass like a dream.

MARION.   Ah, auntie, but those slaves of ours !   Their midnight revels drive sleep from my eyes.   The click of glasses, the shuffle of cards, the rattle of dice, all terrify me. I dread every moment to hear their laughter change to oaths and curses.   To be freed from this life of torture, I would gladly exchange wealth and comfort for poverty and peace.

MRS. M.   It's not a pleasant prospect as viewed by your young eyes.   But when one has buried three husbands, as I have, all of whom went to their graves preserved in alcohol, it looks very much as if *that* was the way of the world, and sobriety the exception.   But you haven't had my experience.

MARION.   Not with husbands, auntie.   But I have had the bitter cup always before my eyes.   My father made his money by the traffic.   My mother died when I was too young to remember her, and until you came to live with us two years ago I gave it little thought.   But then I saw a change in my father : before genial and kind, though never loving to me, he then became what you see him now, stern and fretful, and on the least provocation angry and cruel. Ah ! 'tis the future I dread.   What is in store for us ?

MRS. M.   For you, a good husband and a happy home, I hope.   You deserve it.   For him — Well, he's his own master now, and must have his fling.   He shall have a piece of my mind, and that very soon ; and, if he *is* your father, he shall not abuse you.

MARION. I do not fear him, auntie : 'tis the other, Herbert Poole —

MRS. M. The fat chicken your father and the major are trying to pluck. Why do you fear him ?

MARION. He has spoken to me several times in a way I cannot mistake.

MRS. M. Just as I thought. He admires you, any one can see that. He's a great catch : his father's a millionnaire, and he an only child. He's going to ask you to be his wife.

MARION. No, no, not that ! I could not be happy as his wife. I hope he will never ask me.

MRS. M. But he will, and you are a foolish girl if you refuse him.

MARION. It would be wicked to accept a man I cannot love. So I'll trust the old proverb, " Better a fool than a knave."

(Enter C. JESSIE.)

JESSIE. Ha, ha, ha ! such a racket ! Students forever ! There are those four college fellows who came down here to help in the dining-room, lounging on the rocks, while poor old Pete is frantically waving a napkin from the window of the pantry in which they have locked him. There's music in the air, mammy, such a lark ! *(Sits* R.)

MRS. M. Jessie Morris, haven't I forbidden you to use slang ?

JESSIE. 'Spec' you have, mammy ; but it's the proper caper in polite language, and so stunning ! Besides, my Charlie is a slanguist ; and you've often told me, with tears in your eyes, to pattern my conduct after his.

MRS. M. " Stunning ! " " Slanguist ! " Jessie, you'll drive me wild. And " your Charlie ! " Is that the way to speak of a gentleman whom you expect to marry?

JESSIE. Whom I — expect — I expect to marry. Not much ! Charlie is the awfully expectant one. I'm the " hope deferred *which* maketh the heart sick ; " and if that delicate organ in his susceptible bosom hasn't been stirred by all the ills that hearts are heir to. I've missed my calling.

MRS. M. You little torment ! You don't deserve such a lover.

JESSIE.   No? I'm determined he shall deserve me. He's only on approbation anyway, like a piece of goods sent home from the store; if not suitable, packed off. He's on probation, undergoing a series of tests of affection.

MARION.   If he succeeds, what then?

JESSIE.   Oh! I'll give him some more.

MRS. M.   Take care, child: you may go too far, and lose him.

JESSIE.   Ha, ha, ha! lose my Charlie! never: he's hooked fast. I'm only following the advice of Richard Bell, the best boatman on the coast: "When you've hooked your fish, don't be in a hurry to land him: play him a little; it weakens him, and he won't flounder when he's taken off."

MRS. M.   The idea of treating Charles Wilkins as you would a fish!

JESSIE.   Why not? Didn't you tell me, when Gale Hooker sacked me, that he was a scaly fellow?

MRS. M.   Jessie Morris! I never —

JESSIE.   Oh, yes you did, mammy! that was your rather slangy remark, and that there were as good fish in the sea as ever were caught.

MRS. M.   Well, what of it?

JESSIE.   Then Charlie came along, and you said he was (excuse the slang) a great catch.

MRS. M.   I never —

JESSIE.   Yes, you did, mammy; and if I only angled right I might scoop him.

MRS. M.   Jessie Morris!

JESSIE.   And then *he* asked me to drop him a line when I arrived. Oh, I'm right, mammy! Charlie's very much like a fish: he's too fresh.

MRS. M.   Jessie Morris, drop that slang. If I hear any more of it, I shall shout.

JESSIE (*jumps up*).   Ha, ha, ha!

> Who taught my youthful lips the way
> To catch the slanguage of the day?
> Why, she, the matron I obey, —
>   My mammy.

O Mrs. Morris! it's no use pressing your lips: you have shouted, and you're just as bad as any of us. I blush for you. (*Sits* R.)

(*Bell rings* L.)

MARION. Father's bell! where's Uncle Pete?

PETE (*outside*). Now you jes' min' what I tole you: ef you lock me inter dat yar pantry agin, I'll raise der roof, — mind, raise der roof. (*Enters* R.)

MRS. M. Pete, what's the trouble now?

PETE. Same ole trubble, missis, now and for ebber. Dem ar four stujents jes' shook dar unibersitary, an' wid dar heads full ob Greek and Latin roots, come down year to be waiters. Jes' fool demselves, fool demselves. Why — why, dey don't know nuffin 'bout der tic-tacs ob de waitah; der — der abolitions ob genius dat mark der waitah; der nerve, der consequential misdemeanor ob der waitah — ain't got der gall. Den dar table etiquate, jes' look at it! Put de fork ober to de right ob de plate, an' de knife ober de lef'; stick de biggest kin' ob a graby-spoon into de sugar-bowl, an' de carbing-knife into de butter, an' call dat settin' a table. Jes' sets me wild! I tole 'em 'twas no use, waiters are born, not made, and dey'd better drop ebery ting and hump demselves. (*Crash outside* R.)

JESSIE. They're evidently taking your advice.

PETE (*looking off* R.) Now jes' look a' dar! Dat ar stujent drapped somefin; and dar he stands, wid a tear in his eye, lookin' down on der remains. No blue-blood waitah would do dat.

JESSIE. What would he do, Uncle Pete?

PETE. When de dishes decomposed demselves onto de flo', he'd vamoose into de pantry libely.

JESSIE. Yes, "scatter the chink, and leave others to think."

PETE. Den dey's lackin' in modesty, dat crown ob glory in a waitah. When a gent calls "Waitah," free or four ob dem stujents jes' rush pell-mell, as if dey was gwine to a fire or de fus' table at a barbecue. No fus'-family waitah does dat. (*Imitates.*) At de fus' call he lays his years back, looks pleasant if he kin, and listens; at de second call, opens his eyes, and looks wild; at de third, moves slowly and gracefully ob coorse, towards de suppliant fur his bounty. At de fourfe, he's at his elbow wid a gentle, "Call sar, yes sar." It's no use: must presarbe de dignity ob de profesh, or de whole structure ob s'ciety am underdone.

JESSIE. "One to make ready, two to prepare, three to go

slam-bang," four you is dar.   Ha, ha, ha! Uncle Pete, you
are the *beau idéal* of a servitor.

PETE.   Miss Jessie, I aint much of a beau, an'—an' I don't
idle much; but I'se been servin' fer upwards of twenty years,
an' I's sumfin ob a canooser if dat is what you mean.   (*Bell
rings* L.)

MARTIN (*outside* L.).   Pete, Pete, you rascal!

PETE.   O Lor'! dat bell, an' I foolin' here!   (*Crosses to
door* L.)

JESSIE.   Uncle Pete.

PETE.   Yas, Miss Jessie.

JESSIE.   He's only rung twice: lay back your ears, open
your eyes, and look wild.   "We must preserbe de dignity
ob de profesh."

PETE.   Dat's so in de abstract; but de han' dat pulls dat
yar bell am mighty apt to pull wool, an' in dat abstraction
dignity don't count.   (*Exit* L.)

JESSIE (*jumping up*).   What's the programme to-day,
Marion?

MARION.   I have nothing to propose, Jessie: I shall be
very quiet.

JESSIE.   Oh dear! that won't suit me.   The idea of coming down here to be quiet!   It's monstrous.   It's an insult to
that beautiful sea, in constant motion.   Quiet! not for me,
thank you.   Sailing gayly over the waters, climbing and
scrambling among the rocks, swimming and diving amid the
surf, dancing and waltzing with moonlight and music till
midnight, and waking in the morning with a headache,—
that's seaside life.   I can manage all but the dancing: there
are no fellows.   Yes, we've the students to fall back upon.
I'll just raid the kitchen, and set them up for a fandango this
very night.

MRS. M.   You'll do nothing of the kind, Jessie.   A pack
of waiters!   What would Mr. Wilkins say?

JESSIE.   He'd say I was a jolly girl for taking care of his
friends.   Charlie's one of them: he's a student.

MRS. M.   He'd feel flattered at being classed as a waiter.

JESSIE.   He is a waiter, a patient waiter—for me.

MRS. M.   You'll do very well without any masculine society.   Imitate Marion, and enjoy a little quiet.

JESSIE.   Marion, indeed!   I'm sure she longs just as much
as I do for the advent of one good able-bodied gentlemanly
fellow to break the monotony of our present existence.

MARION. I wish for your sake, Jessie, a dozen such would appear; but, as for me, I would not care if I never saw a man again.

JESSIE. When a girl talks like that, be sure she is just heart-sick for the presence of somebody in particular, whom her imagination and a pair of high-heeled boots have lifted a little higher than ordinary masculine mortals.

(JEROME *appears* C.)

JEROME. May I come in?

JESSIE. And there he is! (*Sits* R.)

MARION (*jumping up*). Mr. Jerome! is it possible?

JEROME (*comes down, and takes* MARION'S *hand*). Judge for yourself; happy to meet you again. What a color the sea is giving you! (*Turns and shakes hands with* JESSIE, *who rises.*) Ah, Miss Jessie! this is the place for you.

JESSIE. Now that a real man has come, yes.

JEROME (*crosses, and shakes hands with* MRS. MORRIS). And how is my old opponent of the card-table? Mrs. Morris, whenever I think of you, my ears tingle.

MRS. M. A guilty conscience, Mr. Jerome. It was very kind of you to look us up. Marion was just wishing you —

MARION. Auntie!

JESSIE. Mother!

MRS. M. Now, what's the matter? — Wishing you success in your new enterprise. No harm in that, is there?

JEROME. Certainly not. (*To* MARION) I shall prize the kind regard as a happy omen of coming victory. (*All sit;* MRS. M. *on lounge,* JEROME L. *of table,* MARION R. *of table,* JESSIE *chair* R.) Rambling about the piazza, and seeing your doors open, I ventured to speak. It's rather early for a call: hope I'm not in the way?

MARION. No, indeed. Then, you are stopping here?

JEROME. For the present, yes. I'm down here on business; rather a romantic sort.

JESSIE. Romantic? Looking for a wife?

MRS. M. More likely, a divorce case.

JEROME. Both wrong. I'm looking for a missing millionnaire.

MRS. M. A millionnaire! This is a queer place to look for him.

JEROME. Yes; but he's about here, I'm certain. It is my good fortune to be the partner of an old friend of my father, who is trying to lift me into the profession through his position and influence. Twenty years ago he one day received in his office an old acquaintance, whom he had not seen for years. On this occasion he was accompanied by a little girl five or six years of age. He announced himself as a returned Californian, who had lost his wife on the passage home. His errand was to get Mr. Perkins to take charge of his funds, some ten thousand dollars, for investment, while he was seeking a home for his child. He left his money, departed, and has never been seen from that time.

MRS. M. And the money?

JEROME. Was carefully invested, and re-invested with always increasing returns; so that now, with houses, stocks, and lands, the unknown, if he is found, will be a very wealthy man.

MARION. It must be the missing Nathan Roberts.

MRS. M. Whom you read about just now.

JEROME. Exactly. That advertisement has appeared year' after year without any application for the reward. The addition of my name to the advertisement seems to have brought good luck; for three days ago an old Californian imparted the pleasing intelligence that he had seen and recognized the missing man in this place. With this clew I am here to hunt up the lost one, with the Californian as a companion. Unfortunately the bar-room here has proved too great an attraction for my witness: he became beastly intoxicated, and I am obliged to wait the termination of his spree. So you see, ladies, I am out of business and in for pleasure. By the way, Miss Jessie, I came round in a yacht, and had for company Mr. Charles Wilkins.

JESSIE. My Charlie! Where is he?

JEROME. The fact is, Charlie is not the sailor one would have imagined from his appearance and demeanor on starting out. He is now on board recovering from a severe attack of sea-sickness, and unwilling to trust himself in the small boat to come ashore.

JESSIE. Ha, ha, ha! that's just like Charlie: he's a splendid sailor on shore, but out to sea, oh, my! he's all at sea.

JEROME (*rising*). Suppose we go and look him up.

MARION (*rising*). I should be delighted. Come, Jessie.

JESSIE. No, I thank you: I'm not prepared to look him

up, or look up to him, in his present condition. If he wants me, here I am.

JEROME. Ready to receive him with open arms. Be kind to him, Jessie, for Charlie Wilkins is one of the best fellows I know.

JESSIE. Is he? I'd no idea your acquaintance was so limited.

JEROME (*to* MRS. MORRIS). Will you accompany us?

MRS. M. (*rising quickly*). I should be pleased —

JESSIE. Um, um. (*Making faces and gestures she is to stay.*)

MRS. M. Did you speak, Jessie?

JESSIE (*with gestures as before;* JEROME *and* MARION *converse apart*). You're not going to leave me alone?

MRS. M. (*looking first at* JEROME, *and then at* JESSIE). I should be pleased to (*sits*) some other time.

JEROME (*crosses to* JESSIE). You shall not be left alone. (*Takes her hand.*) Good girl, I owe you one, and I'll go find him. (*To* MARION.) Shall we start, Miss Moore?

MARION. I am quite ready. (*They go up and off piazza* R., *conversing*).

MRS. M. Now, I'd like to know what all that telegraphing was for.

JESSIE. Don't you see they are in love? Didn't you notice what a color the *sea* gave her when she saw him?

MRS. M. In love? They in love? What will your uncle say?

JESSIE. If he is wise, he will say nothing; if otherwise, there'll be an explosion.

MARTIN (*outside* L.). Start yourself, quick! (PETE *tumbles in from* L.; *door slammed.*)

JESSIE. Something like that.

PETE. Der ole man's a little feveish dis mornin'. Can't do nuffin' wid him. He won't git up, he won't lie down; but he jest rolls hisself about on de ragged edge ob dispair, rehearsing der hole book ob Lamentations. Said der wa'nt nobody in de wide world lobed him, and I standin' dar all de time. I tole him he was mistook, an' I said, "Yas, dar is, Massa Moore; I don't keer if you is white, I lubs you as if you was my own brudder." Dat kinder mollified him, roused him, fired him, an — an — he fired me fro' de door. (*Crosses to* R.) I'se tender feelin's, an de least ting moves me; jes' de liftin' ob a number nine boot startles me el:ery time. (*Exit* R.)

MRS. M. (*rises*). I'll go and see what's the trouble. (*Exit* L.)

JESSIE. So Charlie's here! I thought he wouldn't stay away long; that not even his dread of the sea would prevent his obeying my express order that if he came he must come by water, and in a yacht too, which of all things he detests. I'd like to have seen his face when they struck rough water. Ha, ha, ha!

CHARLIE (*outside* C., *sings*).

> "We sail the waters blue,
> And our saucy ship's a beauty."

(*Appears door* C.) Ahoy! ahoy there! (*Hitches his trousers, sailor fashion.*) Ah, my — my darling! (*Comes down staggering.*) "The sweet little cherub who sits up aloft" (*catches at table*) — steady, steady!

JESSIE. Charlie, have you been drinking?

CHARLIE. Drinking, Jessie? you know that's not one of my faults.

JESSIE. But you pitch about so!

CHARLIE (*catches table*). That's the peculiar nautical roll which one acquires from familiarity with the deep. Yachting, Jessie, is glorious: you've no idea what fun there is in it. (*Aside.*) Fun for the boys. (*Aloud.*) You should have seen me at the helm, grasping the — what is it, — and shouting my orders: "Belay there, belay! Haul taut that jib. Let go the main sheet. Heave to, and clap on more sail!" and then the ecstasy of feeling yourself slipping through the water at the rate of forty hours a knot. No, not that, but knotty forts — pshaw!

JESSIE. Skip the knots, Charlie.

CHARLIE. And then to lean lazily over the side, and gaze far down into the depths of ocean, and feel as if you were throwing your — your —

JESSIE. Boots, Charlie?

CHARLIE. "Soul" was the word I was seeking, Miss Morris.

JESSIE. Well, I helped you to a pair of them. But, Charlie, was all this before you turned in, or after?

CHARLIE. Turned in?

JESSIE. When you were afraid one moment you were going to die, and the next that you wasn't. O Charlie! it's no use trying to carry sail: you don't know the tiller from a tar-bucket. The log of your last voyage has been overhauled, and you are set down as a stowaway, neither useful nor ornamental; ha, ha, ha! Mr. Jerome has been here, Charlie.

CHARLIE. He has? Then the nautical craze is over.

JESSIE. And one more test of affection — I can't say you were able to stand that test, Charlie — turned in to your account.

CHARLIE. Isn't it about time that account was settled, Miss Morris? Don't you think I've been making a fool of myself, for your sake, quite long enough?

JESSIE. Not quite, Charlie.

CHARLIE. I do. Allow me to call your attention to the dangers I have encountered by sea and land, at your instigation.

JESSIE. Go on: I do like a blood-curdling romance.

CHARLIE. Romance? Great Scott!

JESSIE. Well, he was a romancer: beat him if you can.

CHARLIE. When, in the exuberance of the unfolding of a youthful affection, I flung myself at your feet last summer at the mountains, and swore you were the only woman I had ever loved —

JESSIE. Your own original remarks.

CHARLIE. You transported me with the declaration that my attentions were not altogether distasteful to you. You further told me, that, could I stand the several tests of affection to which you *always* subjected your admirers, you — you — would see about it.

JESSIE. Well, that was fair, wasn't it?

CHARLIE. Fair? If I had caught at that time an idea of what your previous admirers had attempted, I should have sought the place where you bury your victims, picked out a soft place, and taken a rest.

JESSIE. A soft place! Why, you are running ahead —

CHARLIE. Miss Morris!

JESSIE. Of your story. Proceed.

CHARLIE. I consented, and calmly awaited your first test. It came with a rush. Seated on the piazza of the hotel one morning I was aroused by the rattle of wheels and frantic cries of "Help! help!" Looking down the road, I saw a galloping horse with a buggy behind him, and in that buggy you. I rushed down, seized the animal by the bits, and the next moment found myself rolling in the dust. When I recovered my equilibrium, and had cleared my ears of dust, you were trotting leisurely away, shouting —

JESSIE. Ha, ha, ha! a test of affection, Charlie.

CHARLIE. Exactly. On another occasion, the same cries for "Help, help!" directed my attention seaward to an overturned boat, a mile from shore, to the keel of which you were clinging. Heedless of my apparel, I plunged into the water, and after a tough swim reached the boat just in time to see you in bathing costume leisurely swim shoreward, while I had to cling to the keel until somebody came and took me in.

JESSIE. Didn't I come after you? Didn't I take you in?

CHARLIE. You did, — twice the same day. Then there was the great bull-fight. At that time you were deeply interested in the exploits of the hero of a then popular romance, "The Matador of Madrid." Inspired with admiration for that reckless "son of merry Spain," you were anxious I should emulate his exploits, become an amateur matador, and attack a bovine of the masculine gender, who was monarch of all he surveyed in a pasture adjoining the hotel. In the particular state of ecstasy in which I then found myself, I would have attacked a boiling locomotive and driven it from the track at your command: so, with your red shawl floating from my left hand, and with a pitchfork grasped in my right, I leaped the fence, and faced the bull.

JESSIE. Boldly and fearlessly.

CHARLIE. To all appearance, yes. There *was* a slight disturbance just under my ribs; but I faced his majesty, whom I was about to despatch *à la matador*, and shouted, "Come on!" Of course no well-trained bull could resist such an invitation: he came on. There was a confusion of horns, pitchfork, shawl, and matador, one wild bellow, several terrific yells, and a cyclone into which I was hurled. I came down somewhere in the next county, and retired from the matador business forever.

JESSIE. You stood that test well. Any thing more?

CHARLIE. That, with your last attempt to bring me round by water, completes the programme. If I live to relate my experience, it's because I was born under a lucky star. It's a wonder to me you have not sent me to stand up before some of those bruisers of Madison Square.

JESSIE. Oh, I never thought of that!

CHARLIE (*quickly*). Then, don't.

JESSIE. That would be not only a test of affection, but of endurance.

CHARLIE (*aside*). What a fool I was to mention it! (*Aloud.*) Don't think of it for a moment: any thing but that!

JESSIE. Then, I'll give you an easy one.

CHARLIE. Insatiate damsel, give me no more. I've been bruised and battered fighting your windmills. Let me rest a while by your side, and — and — spoon.

JESSIE. Speaking of spoons, Charlie, do you know that four of your college fellows are in this hotel, engaged in rattling those useful table articles?

CHARLIE. Oh, yes! some of our fellows on a lark. Doing well, ain't they?

JESSIE. So well, Charlie, that I am anxious to see you at the same occupation.

CHARLIE. Me! see me waiting on tables! Well, I like that.

JESSIE. I knew you would.

CHARLIE. Miss Morris, I respectfully but firmly decline.

JESSIE. I have set my heart upon it.

CHARLIE. Then, the quicker you take your heart off its ridiculous resting-place, and restore it to its original setting, the better for your health and my future happiness.

JESSIE. Ah! but you'll do it all the same. It shall be another test of affection.

CHARLIE. Test be — blest! Understand me, Miss Morris, I am your humble servant to command in any thing reasonable; but as for girding my waist with a white apron, and being the humble servant at the beck and call of every loafer who wants a fish-dinner or a clam-bake, never!

JESSIE. Oh, yes, you will, Charlie!

CHARLIE. By the great horn spoon —

JESSIE. That sounds like a waiter's oath.

CHARLIE (*turning up stage*). Good-morning, Miss Morris.

JESSIE. Where are you going?

CHARLIE. Back to town.

JESSIE. By water?

CHARLIE. By rail, the shortest and fastest route.

JESSIE. Well, good-by.

CHARLIE. Forever. (*Going.*)

JESSIE. By the way, Charlie, you spoke of bringing down an engagement ring.

CHARLIE (*returns*). I have brought it, but —

JESSIE. You might leave it with one of the college boys, for I'm sure a collegian in a white apron will be the man of my choice.

CHARLIE. That settles it. Where is the keeper of this shebang? I'll engage myself for waiter, cook, scullion, bootblack, any thing, as a test of affection, bah! (*Exit* R.)

JESSIE. Ha, ha, ha! Poor Charlie! (*Rises.*) Won't there be a smash among the crockery? I'll follow, and see the sport: they'll be sure to haze the *fresh* man. (*Exit* R.)

MARTIN (*outside* L.). What are you talking about? (*Enters* L., *followed by* MRS. MORRIS.) I'm surely old enough to take care of myself, to know my own mind.

MRS. M. Too old to make a fool of yourself, carousing night after night, at your time of life.

MARTIN. Shut up!

MRS. M. Shut up! I wish you were, where you belong, in an insane-asylum. Do you think I'm blind? Though you call yourself rich, I tell you no fortune can stand such plunges as you are making into yours. Your health is broken: you are peevish, fretful, and ugly. Shut up, indeed! A pretty way to talk to your sister! Mark my words, Martin Moore: if you don't turn square round, and break off in your evil courses, your funeral is set down for no distant day. Shut up, indeed! (*Exit* L.)

MARTIN (*sitting* L. *of table*). She's right: I am breaking up. Oh, my head! my head! Rich, indeed! I've had a run of bad luck that has nearly swamped me, — so bad that I don't see how I am to get away from this hotel without help. Now, here's a quarrel with my sister, whose bank-account might have helped me. Curse the luck!

(*Enter* MAJOR FITZPATRICK, R.)

MAJOR. Are ye there, Martin, me by?

MARTIN. Hallo, Fitz! how's your head?

MAJOR (*sits* R. *of table*). Jist shplittin', me by. Bad luck to the owld punkin! it's howldin' a wake over the remains of the late merry Major Fitzpatrick. Oh! it's moighty illigant, the faste of rason, and the flow of sowl, an' the jig's a loively one while the glasses are dancin' and the corks bobbin'. But whin you've to play the piper for that same jig the nixt mornin' wid the Divil's own tattoo batin' forninst yer skull, you've no ear to kape stip wid the music, me by.

MARTIN. Grumbling, you old toper? Have you seen snakes this morning?

MAJOR. Niver a shnake.' Spakin' ov the varmints, do you mind the shtory, that St. Patrick druv the last shnake in Ould Oireland int' a chist, double locked the front dure, and tossed him into the say?

MARTIN. I've heard the story.

MAJOR. It's all a mishtake, me by: it was a whiskey-cask he druv him into, wid his legs shtickin' out of the bung-hole. An' he didn't drop into the say at all at all; for he's been walkin' op and down the earth iver since, as many a poor fellow can tistify, who's looked afther him wid shtrong glasses.

MARTIN. Old man! what's the matter with you?

MAJOR. I'm jist afther ruminatin' a bit. That same shnake must have had a powerful soakin', for he's been in liquor iver since.

MARTIN. I wish he was in yours.

MAJOR. Faith, I'm thinkin' we'll both wake up some foine mornin' in toime to say the tail ind of the procession. Well, we've had a merry-go-round since we fust clinked glasses, twinty years ago, at "The Flowing Bowl."

MARTIN. Hush! don't speak that name here.

MAJOR. Martin, me by, you're not goin' back on the old sign where you first made money?

MARTIN. You know there are reasons why my life at that place should not be too carefully looked into.

MAJOR. You mane the little shindy we had one night wid a stranger. He flung a glass at you: it missed, and shtruck his little girl. Oh, murder, what a night! We were all blind drunk.

MARTIN. The stranger fled, the child died of its injuries.

MAJOR. So you've often towld me.

MARTIN. I wouldn't like to have my daughter hear of this, it might distress her: so be careful how you allude to (*looks round*) "The Flowing Bowl." Where did we leave off last night?

MAJOR. Where we began, me by, — wid whiskey.

MARTIN. Pshaw! I mean at cards.

(HERBERT POOLE *lounges in*, C., *and listens*.)

MAJOR. I've an indishtinct recollection that we left off at cards moighty oftin to lubricate our fingers wid a shmell at the bottle.

MARTIN. And so lost our heads. Fitz, we have been playing a losing game with Herbert Poole. We thought we had in him a young and inexperienced fellow, rich in funds and with great expectations, whom two old hands like ourselves could easily make pay roundly for his experience. But we are outwitted at every point. He keeps his head, and rakes the pile, while we —

MAJOR. Allow our social instincts to rise superior to the love of filthy lucre. Doesn't the woise man say, " Betther a bowl of smokin' punch than a faste of dry chips"? Bedad! Let him rake the chips : we'll cool our mortification wid the hot punch.

MARTIN. Do you know how we stand ?

MAJOR. Together, me by, as long as we can shtand! and whin we fall, faith, we'll take a drop together.

MARTIN. Fitz, be serious if you can. We must find some way to raise money. I'm dead broke.

MAJOR. You don't mane it, me by ?

MARTIN. I must know at once how I stand with Herbert Poole.

POOLE (*at back of table*). And so you shall, Martin my boy.

MARTIN. Poole !

MAJOR. Ah ! the top uv the morning to ye's, my boy.

POOLE (*comes down* R.). Major, I'm glad to see you sitting up this morning: the last I saw of you was under the table, doubled up.

MAJOR. Doubled op, indade ! Faith, ye's eyesight must have been a bit onsteady, to have seen two of me to onct.

POOLE (*sitting* R.). Gentlemen, I heard a remark, as I entered the room, touching our financial standing. I think I can enlighten you (*takes out pocket-book*): I have just been looking over my memoranda, and find, Major, several I O U's of yours, the total footing of which is thirty-two hundred dollars.

MAJOR. Thirty-two ! Begorra, there's a mishtake in the figgers. How would I owe the loikes of what I niver had ?

POOLE. There is no mistake: that is the footing.

MAJOR. If that's the footing, I've not a financial leg to shtan' upon, me by.

POOLE. You can settle at your convenience.

MAJOR. Faith, an' I will, I'm obleeged to ye's.

POOLE. You, Martin Moore, are my debtor in the sum of sixty-eight hundred.

MARTIN. You are crazy, Poole! I owe you no such sum.

POOLE. Here are the documents, your signature —

MARTIN. I've been swindled, outrageously swindled!

POOLE. No, you have been fairly beaten at your own game. You thought 'I was young and inexperienced, a chicken to be plucked by two bold hawks. Remember, it was you who proposed the game, not I. You would have taken my money if you could. Luck was against you, and I take yours.

MAJOR (*rises*). It's my opinion, Martin, that for a shmall baste, the chicken has a moighty long bill. (*Turns up stage.*)

POOLE. Will you give me your check?

MARTIN. If that will satisfy you, yes. But it would be worthless.

POOLE. Worthless?

MARTIN. Yes; for I have no funds to meet it. I am ruined. (*Head in hands.*)

POOLE (*crosses to chair*, R. *of table*). Not quite, Martin: you have a daughter.

MARTIN. Well?

POOLE. Give her to me, and we are quits.

MARTIN. Would you ruin her as you have me?

POOLE. She shall be a queen of society, wealthy, courted, admired. I would make her my wife.

MARTIN. Your wife? You mean it?

POOLE. On her wedding-day, — provided I am her husband, of course, — I will not only cancel your indebtedness to me, but I will place to your credit ten thousand dollars.

MARTIN (*aside*). His wife! Here's luck! (*Aloud.*) Poole, she is yours (*shakes hands*). I couldn't hope for a better future for my daughter. Fitz, do you hear?

MAJOR. Faith, I'm listhening wid both ears wide open toight. Loike myself, you have sittled your account at your own convaniance. But suppose your proposed quane of society declines the honor.

MARTIN. She dare not. My will is law in her case. I never go back on my word.

MAJOR. Faith, it's betther than your I O U's, thin. But you wouldn't force her, me by.

MARTIN. She shall marry Poole if I have to drag her to the altar.

MAJOR. By the blissed St. Pathrick, no! You may thry moral swasion: I'm only opposed to that on timperance principles. But she's a swate girl, and she shall marry whom she loikes. If it's not Poole, your fat's in the foire, and I'm jist the by to kick over the stew-pan.

MARTIN. Fitz, you're drunk.

MAJOR. At tin o'clock in the mornin'? Thin it's a dhry drunk, and don't count.

POOLE. By what right do you interfere, you miserable sot?

MAJOR. Will, niver you moind, Misther Poole. I've a shtrong wakeness for fair play —

MARTIN. Oh! Fitz is all right, he won't interfere. There shall be no violence with Marion.

MAJOR. Kape to that, and I'm dumb.   .

POOLE. Then, I may speak to Miss Moore with your permission?

MARTIN. Certainly. I will speak to her now. (*Exit* L.)

MAJOR (*comes down, and sits* L. *of table*). Now, me by, a word wid you. You jist now complimented me with the title of miserable sot. I moight have shtood the last word, for I know my own wakeness in the matther of shtrong drink, but I'm blissed if I'll be made miserable by the loikes of you.

POOLE. Do you want to quarrel with me?

MAJOR. Sure, I'm a man of pace at any price.

POOLE. Bah! you've picked up something that you want to sell.

MAJOR. I picked meself op from onder the table this mornin', and wid meself that (*throws a dice on table*).

POOLE. Ah! one I dropped. (*About to take it.*)

MAJOR (*clapping his hand on it*). Don't touch it, me by: it's loaded.

POOLE (*starting back, and looking at* MAJOR). Loaded? How did you find that out?

MAJOR. I've tried it, me by; and it's sixes ivery toime.

Moighty convenient for a chate, a shwindler, and a black-guard loike Herbert Poole.

POOLE (*starting up*). Major Fitzpatrick!

MAJOR. Kape your sate: the truth shouldn't froighten you. By the by, those I O U's of mine, I'd loike to look at thim.

POOLE. For what purpose?

MAJOR. Curiosity, me by.

POOLE (*hands papers*). Here they are.

MAJOR. If it's all the same to you, me by, I'll kape them for the convaniance of knowin' how much I owe you, to refrish me memory occasionally. Afther that—

POOLE. Well?

MAJOR. I'll burn them, me by.

POOLE. You will return that dice?

MAJOR (*rises*). I'll think about it, me by. (*Going* R.) Faith, I'll not. (*Aside.*) Thrust an Irishman for luck! It's not his at all at all, and divil a six can I throw wid it. But niver moind, he's not the fust blackguard who's been shot wid an unloaded gun. (*Exit* R.)

POOLE. What unlucky chance made me drop that dice? The Irishman has me in his clutches, and my magic throw is powerless.

(*Enter* MARTIN, L.)

MARTIN. She's not in her room. (MARION *and* JEROME *appear on piazza.*) Ah, there she is! Marion, come here.

MARION. You'll excuse me, Mr. Jerome?

JEROME. Certainly. (*Lifts his hat, and exit* R.)

MARION (*comes down*). Well, father?

MARTIN. My friend Mr. Poole is waiting to speak with you. (*Exit* L.)

MARION (L.). To speak with me? Mr. Poole, I am all attention.

POOLE (R.). Miss Moore, you must have seen that I have long admired you. When I tell you that admiration has deepened into love, you will not be surprised that I take the first opportunity, after obtaining your father's consent, to ask you to be my wife.

MARION. I am not surprised, Mr. Poole: 'tis what I have been expecting. I decline the honor.

POOLE. Miss Moore, have you considered my position in society? As my wife you would move in the first circles. My family—

MARION. Is of the best. I understand that. But I am
not seeking position : you offer yourself, and that is an ob-
jection. You are a bold, dissipated man ; no woman could be
happy as your wife, did she love you; and as your attentions
have not affected me in that way, you must excuse me.

POOLE. I confess I am a little wild, but marriage will reform all that: will you not aid the good work?

MARION. I will aid any good work that promises success, but the experiment of marrying a man to reform him
has seldom had that happy result.

POOLE. Your father looks upon my proposal kindly: I
fear you will greatly disappoint him if you persist in your
refusal.

MARION. Perhaps my father's wealth has influenced your
offer.

POOLE. So little, that when I tell you he is not only poor,
but deeply in debt, you will understand that I have no mer-
cenary motives.

MARION. Poor! And in debt? To you perhaps?

POOLE. Precisely.

MARION. Debts of the gaming-table. I see it all. This
marriage is to settle his indebtedness to you. Once more I
decline.

POOLE. Take a little time to consider it, Miss Moore. I
knew you would be hard to win. I did not expect you to
fall into my arms at the first proposal, and your opposition
only increases my desire to make you my wife. I shall still
hope. I am young, of good birth, passably good-looking,
and have fine prospects. I foresee that you and your father
will find hard lines in the future. I shall patiently await my
time. I admire you, love you, would be a devoted husband.
Think of this, and when you need me command me. Good-
morning. (*Exit* R.)

MARION. My father ruined! can he speak the truth?
(*Crosses to* R.)

(*Enter* MARTIN, L.)

MARTIN. Well, girl, is it all settled?

MARION. It is: I have refused him.

MARTIN. Refused him? Herbert Poole! Then you
have ruined me.

MARION. I do not love him.

MARTIN. Romantic twaddle!

MARION. I cannot respect him.

MARTIN. Stuff and nonsense! Feather your nest first; and all the respect, the billing and cooing, will come after marriage.

MARION. I will not, can not, marry that man.

MARTIN (*fiercely*). Will not! You shall. Do you suppose I have kept you on my hands all these years, made a lady of you, surrounded you with luxury and comfort, to be defied by you at the very moment I need your help?

MARION. My help?

MARTIN (*tenderly*). O Marion, don't disappoint me now! I have tried to be a good father to you: help me now, for we are beggars. Every thing — gold, houses, lands — has slipped through my fingers. With this marriage, all may be regained: without, the future is a life of poverty and privation.

MARION. I *will* help you. I will work, slave, for your comfort. I will welcome the poverty if it bring us peace, if it takes us out of this wild, wicked life of folly that is full of terror; any thing but marry that man.

MARTIN (*fiercely*). Curse your peace and poverty! Do you think I'll grovel among the beggars, when a word from you can lift us above all fear for the future? You shall marry that man. Balk me in this (*seizes her wrist*), and I'll strangle you!

MARION. Father, you are hurting me.

(*Enter* MAJOR, R.)

MAJOR. Martin, me by, will you ate? (MARION *crosses to lounge, on which she sinks, burying her face in the pillow*.) Beyant there's as foine a bafeshteak as iver roamed the broad peraries of the Wist, havin' a quiet smoke on the table wid a dish of rael maley petates, Irish to the backbone, jist rowlin' back their nightcaps with a good-mornin' for ye's, and their eyes lookin' for all the world loike a purty girl waitin' for a mash.

MARTIN. Bother eating!

MAJOR. Wid all me heart, me by; but as it's a nissisary avil betwane drinks, we must humor it.

MARTIN. Has the morning mail arrived?

MAJOR. There's a hape of letthers beside your plate, so you can despatch two males to onct.

MARTIN. Come on, then. (*Stoops over* MARION.) Remember, I will be obeyed. (*Crosses to* R.) Come, Fitz. (*Exit* R.)

MAJOR (*looking at* MARION).   Just in toime, Major, me by.
I belave he was about to make a male of the choild.   (*Crosses
to lounge.*)   You seem to be troubled, me darlin'.   Am I to
congratulate Misther Poole —

MARION (*starting up*).   Major Fitzpatrick! do you wish to
insult me?   Are you concerned in this vile plot to make me
share the fortunes of a man whom I detest?   Are you abet-
ting this cruel wrong?

MAJOR.   It's little consarn I have for the ways of mathri-
mony onyhow; and the plot, I'm thinkin', is confined to the
two of thim, the ould man and the by; and if I'm a-bettin', it
is, that the famale parthy in the shuit can whip the both of
thim if she have a moind.

MARION.   O Major! you will aid me, you will be my
friend?

MAJOR.   To be sure I will.   If you could foind a way to
look kindly on this offer, it would be moighty convanient for
the ould man, for he's put to his trumps wid niver a one in
his hand, and this marriage would give us all a lift.   He's
disperate —

MARION.   And so am I.   He has no right to make me
marry this man.   He shall kill me first, as he has threatened.

MAJOR.   Oh, he has threatened, has he?   (*Aside.*)   Martin,
me by, you've broken your parole, your jig's op.   (*Aloud.*)
My darlin', how old moight you bay?

MARION.   Twenty-three.

MAJOR (*looking round*).   Have you any recollection of a
place called (*looking round*) "The Flowing Bowl"?

MARION.   No: my first recollection is of being in a children's hospital.

MAJOR.   Yis, for a faver maybe.

MARION.   I think an accident had happened to me.
From there I was taken to the country, until I was old
enough to go to school, where I was for five years.   I've
been with father ever since.

MAJOR *aside*).   Martin, me by, you're a gay desaver.   The
choild died, did she?   (*Aloud.*)   Your father has no roight
to force you in this matther; and, if he had, he's not your
father.

MARION.   Not my father —

MAJOR.   Aisy, honey!   'tis a sacret he has blabbed in his
cups: as yet I have only his word for it.   I'll watch; an' whin

the wine's in and the wit is out, he may shpring a lake wid his mouth, an' if he does I'l make a tunnel of me ear and catch the drippin's.

MARTIN (*outside* R.). Fitz, Fitz, are you coming?

MAJOR. I'm wid ye, me by.— Kape a good heart, me girl. I've a moind that young lawyer Jerome (don't blush) moight loike to take a hand in this affair.

MARION (*placing her hand on the* MAJOR's *arm*). Major!

MAJOR (*covering her hand with his own*). That's jist the hand he'd loike to hold, I'm thinkin': it's a moighty pretty hand, and would pay the costs of court.

MARTIN (*outside* R.). Fitz, Fitz!

MAJOR. Immagiately, me by (*goes* R.).— Thrust to luck, me darlin', and Major Fitzpatrick. Me breakfast's gettin' cowld, but the owld man will make it hot for me (*Exit* R.)

MARION. Not my father? Impossible! He would not force me to marry if he had not the power to compel obedience, and yet no father who loved his child would consent to such an alliance. But if not his child, who am I? Why this mystery? (JEROME *and* JESSIE *appear, promenading the piazza.*) Perhaps I am a foundling left at his door, perhaps the child of shame. Perhaps — the Major must have dreamed it after one of his midnight carousals. (*Turns up stage, sees* JEROME, *who bows.* MARION *turns back.*) Mr. Jerome, had he been my father's choice, how gladly would I have consented! (JEROME *bows to* JESSIE, *and comes down.*)

JEROME. Miss Moore, Marion — may I not call you by that name? You have been kind enough to congratulate me on my future prospects so earnestly, that in you I feel I have a true friend.

MARION. You have indeed. (*Gives her hand.*)

JEROME (*grasping it warmly*). Marion, I love you; heart and soul acknowledge you as mistress: may I not hope that in that future so bright with promise I shall find you sharing my joys and sorrows as my wife?

MARION. Mr. Jerome, I —(*hesitates*).

JEROME. I have been hasty, I have startled you. I have given you no reason to suspect that I loved you; but it would have been ungenerous in me to seek your hand while struggling with poverty. Now all this is changed, and I can honestly claim the one I have loved from the moment we first met.

(HERBERT POOLE *appears* C.)

MARION. O Mr. Jerome! Clifton —

JEROME (*kissing her hand*). I read my answer in your eyes. May I speak to your father?

MARION (*breaking away*). My father! (*Goes* R.) No, no: he will never consent. What am I about to do? Burden the life of the man I truly love, with a wife whose father is not only a bankrupt, but a gambler and a drunkard; who knows not if she has a right to associate with honest people? No, no! I love him too well for that.

JEROME. Marion?

MARION. It will break my heart, but I will do it: better to sacrifice myself than him. (*Turns, speaks quickly*.) Mr. Jerome, what you ask is impossible. My father has already selected a husband for me. I must obey.

JEROME. A husband for you! Who?

POOLE (*comes down* R.). Herbert Poole, at your service. (*To* MARION.) You consent? (*Holds out his hand*.)

MARION (*after a struggle, places her hand in his*). Yes.

POOLE. Ah! Let me salute my future bride. (*About to kiss her*.)

MARION (*dashes away his hand*). No, no, never. Oh, I shall go mad, mad! (*Runs off* L.)

POOLE (*goes to door* L., *and looks off;* JEROME *leans against table, with arms folded, watching him*). A little coy. Shall I follow her? No, I'll give her time to collect herself. (*Comes down, and faces* JEROME.) My dear fellow, you have my sympathy. You came too late. I have carried off the prize.

JEROME. It strikes me the prize took herself off, my dear fellow.

POOLE. Ah! something of a joker, I see.

JEROME. Possibly. The joker is the best card in the pack, as you should know.

POOLE. Of course you will now desist from your amorous pursuit of Miss Moore.

JEROME. Certainly not: why should I?

POOLE. Because she has accepted me. You heard her answer to my suit?

JEROME. Yes; and I read her answer to mine in the light of her eyes, the true index of a woman's heart.

POOLE. But I have the promise of her hand.

JEROME. I shall have the hand without the promise, some day.

POOLE (*angrily*). You are a cool fellow! Do you know who I am?

JEROME. By report, yes. The son of Archibald Poole, the millionnaire, an honest man who toiled and slaved to acquire a fortune that will be recklessly squandered by a spendthrift son.

POOLE. And who are you?

JEROME. The son of a poor farmer who worked early and late, and impoverished himself, that his boy might be fitted by education to make his way in the world, and comfort his old age, as he will.

POOLE. And do you imagine that you can beat me out of old Moore's daughter, when I have her promise, and the old man is in my power?

JEROME (*aside*). At last I have the clew. (*Aloud.*) I haven't the least doubt of it.

POOLE. Why, you're a crank, fellow.

JEROME. No; but I'm one of the fellows that turn the crank that winds up the career of such a scoundrel as you are —

POOLE. By —

JEROME. Who carries a pack of marked cards in his breast-pocket —

POOLE. You lie —

JEROME. Loaded dice in a secret place —

POOLE. You infernal — (*Puts his hand back to his hip.*)

JEROME (*quickly seizing his arm, raises it, and snatches pistol from his hip-pocket*). And carries a pistol in his hip-pocket. (*Falls back against table.*)

POOLE (*approaching him*). Curse you! I'll kill you.

JEROME (*coolly raising pistol*). Easy, my dear fellow. I hope for your sake it's not loaded, but I'm afraid it is.

POOLE. Curse you for a meddling fool! (*Goes up* C., *turns.*) You'll find that in this game I hold the winning hand.

JEROME. Not while I have the little joker (*tapping pistol*).

POOLE (*at* C. *door*). I marry Marion Moore, remember that. (*Exit.*)

JEROME. Not if I know a true woman's heart. There's evidently a nice little plot here, that the firm of Perkins &

Jerome are in duty bound to unravel. (*Lays pistol on table.*) Marion marry that man? Bless her dear little heart! her woman's wit would find a way to balk him, even at the altar; if not, mine shall. (JESSIE *appears* C.)

JESSIE. O Mr. Jerome, quick, quick! Richard Bell will be murdered.

JEROME. Murdered! (*Goes up.*)

JESSIE. A ruffian is beating him with his own oars.

JEROME. 'Tis my drunken Californian. — Hallo there! hallo! (*Runs off* C., *followed by* JESSIE. *Enter*, R., MARTIN *and* MAJOR FITZPATRICK.)

MARTIN. Understand once for all, I will have no interference in this business. She is my daughter; and if you dare bring up that business of twenty years ago, you will be the sufferer, not I.

MAJOR. Will, I'd loike to know what ye's dhrivin' at, Martin, me by.

MARTIN. There was a sequel to the quarrel, which I kept from you.

MAJOR. Indade, thin, we'll have the saquel to onct. If I'm to be a sufferer, I'd loike to know the nature of me complaint.

MARTIN. When the stranger left the saloon, he was followed by *you*.

MAJOR. I don't remimber that.

MARTIN. You were too drunk to remember any thing. But you did follow him: you were seen following on the wharves. He never returned: but you did, with blood upon your clothes. Fitz, you murdered that man for his money, and threw his body into the dock.

MAJOR. I murther! faith, you're jokin'. I wouldn't kill a fla for his money.

MARTIN. Oh! you were drunk, and didn't know what you were about. It would go hard with you if the matter were sifted. So be careful, and don't meddle in my affairs.

MAJOR. I'm a murderer, am I? I don't fale it a bit. I don't have bad dhrames, and ghosts awakin' me op wid their howlin'. Faith, it's not right: if I am a murtherer, why shouldn't I have the priviliges? I'm thinkin' I'm a fraud. All right, Martin, me by: I'll be a murtherer to suit your convaniance, and you shall let Marion marry whom she loikes to suit mine. So put that in your poipe, and give it a whiff.

MARTIN. Who is her father, if not I?

JEROME (*outside*). Richard Bell, you are safe; lean on me; this way, this way. (*Enters* C., *supporting* RICHARD BELL, *who has a streak of blood on his forehead to show he has been struck.*)

JEROME. Your pardon, Mr. Moore; but this poor fellow has been wounded, and this is the nearest place.

RICHARD (*wildly*). No, no! I say I'm not the man. Let me go, let me go!

JEROME. It's all right, Richard. Sit down. (*Places him in chair* R. *of table.*)

MARTIN (L.). Who is he?

JEROME. A stranger to me until I rescued him from the fury of a rum-crazed fellow who came here with me. Miss Morris called him Richard Bell. He'll be all right soon: he is dazed by the blow he received. I must ask you to look after him, while I secure his assailant. (*Goes up and off* C.)

RICHARD (*lying back in the chair with his eyes closed*). Keep off, keep off! I know you not. We have never met. I'm a poor boatman: what do I know about gold or California? Let go my throat! Help, help!

MAJOR (R.). Bedad, it's chokin' he is, wid thirst. (*Takes flask from his pocket, and places it to* RICHARD'S *mouth*). Here's a reviver, me by.

RICHARD (*dashes it to the floor, and rises*). Accursed stuff, away! It has ruined my life. I had a wife whose happiness it blasted, whose death it wrought; a child, O my child! It made me murder my child. Twenty years have not blotted out that fearful night. (*Sinks back into chair with his eyes closed*).

MARTIN. Twenty years ago! (*Looks at him closely.*) Fitz, it is the stranger.

MAJOR. Whom I murthered, me by. Faith, I towld ye I was a poor hand at sthickin'.

MARTIN (*aside*). Should he be recognized, I am ruined.

RICHARD (*rouses*). No, no! take that rope from my neck. I knew not what I did. (*Starts to his feet.*) Two devils in human shape tempted me, plied me with liquor. (*Backs up stage.*) I am innocent: let the guilty suffer. Two devils (*Glares at* MAJOR.) Ah! there's one! (*Recognizes* MARTIN.) And there's the other!

(*Enter* MARION, L.)

MARION. Father!

RICHARD. Who called father? (*Sees* MARION.) My wife! (*Staggers back, and falls with his arm over piazza-railing.*)

MARTIN. He must not live to speak again. (*Goes up.*) I'll strangle him where he lies.

MAJOR (*intercepting him*). Martin, you are mad!

MARTIN (*struggling with him*). Hands off, I say!

MARION. Father, what would you do?

MAJOR. Murther: I see it in his oye.

MARTIN (*throws* MAJOR *to* R. *He, near table, sees pistol; snatches it*). Ah! short work with burglars. (*Goes up to* RICHARD.) You speak no more. (*Aims pistol;* MARION *shrieks, and sinks on lounge;* JEROME *enters* C., *seizes* MARTIN'S *arm; the pistol explodes;* JEROME *then quickly snatches it.*)

MARION (*rushing up and falling on* JEROME'S *neck*). Clifton, Clifton!

POOLE (*enters* R.). Scoundrel, give me —

JEROME (*with* L. *arm round* MARION, *presents handle of pistol to* POOLE). Pistol? Certainly. You see it *was* loaded.

(*Picture.*)

ACT II. — *Evening of the same day. Scene as before, with addition of moonlight from* R. *across piazza, and in at the windows.*

(*Enter* JESSIE R.)

JESSIE. Ha, ha, ha! such a guy! My Charlie has donned the apron, and is busily engaged — making blunders. Poor fellow! "I saw him but a moment, but methinks I see him now," hurrying across the room with a tureen of chowder; his foot slipped, and he sat down; the tureen flew up, and he had a free lunch. I took it all in, and so did he, I think, for he looked as though he was strangling. Poor Charlie! I must have him in (*rings bell*). He shall serve refreshments for me (*sits* L. *of table*), and take a lesson from Uncle Pete.

(*Enter* PETE, R.)

PETE. Ring, miss?

JESSIE. Send that new waiter to take my order for refreshments.

PETE. What? dat ar' one that come to-day?

JESSIE. Yes.

PETE. Why, why, Miss Jessie, dat ar' Mr. Wilkins, your young man.

JESSIE. I know.

PETE. Why, he, — he's wus' dan all de res': he's broke more crockery dis arternoon dan he can pay for in free months ef it's all stopped out er his wages.

JESSIE. And what are his wages?

PETE. Nuffin de fust year, 'cept 'sperience an' what he picks up, an' dat's mosely crockery in small bits.

JESSIE. Well, send him in.

PETE. In here? No, dat won't do: I'se de bery partic'-lar major-domo ob dis year section, because Massa Moore want de bes'.

JESSIE. Yes; and because you are "de bes'," I want him to take a lesson from you. Uncle Pete, see that he attends to my wants properly: I want him to excel, to rise in de profesh.

PETE. Rise? he's risin' mos' de time from de flo'.

JESSIE. Call him, please.

PETE (*looking off* R.). Dar he goes now! (*Snaps his fingers and beckons, à la head waiter.*) Here, kidminster, kidminster —

JESSIE. Why do you call him that name?

PETE. Dat's what de stujents call him. 'Spec' it's 'cause he's spread onto de flo' mosely.

(*Enter* CHARLIE, R., *in a white apron, napkin on his arm.*)

CHARLIE. Were you snapping your bones at me, old salmagundi?

PETE. Old sallyme which? (*Pompously.*) I'se de custardin dese year 'partments. I'se major-domo. Don't fool yourself wid respect to your s'perior. (*Struts down to* L.) Take de lady's order. Hump yourself, hump yourself.

JESSIE. This way, kidminster.

CHARLIE. That infernal name again! (*Shakes his fist at* PETE.) Look here, old blackberry jam, if you disclose the secrets of the pantry —

PETE. Demean yerself, de lady called.

CHARLIE. O Jessie! this is ridiculous.

PETE. Dat's so, you igronamus. Is dat the way you take a lady's order?

CHARLIE (*chasing* PETE *into* L. *corner*). Open that yawning chasm of yours again, and I'll close it forever.

PETE. Now, now, don't fool, don't fool! 'Twas de lady's 'tickler order, dat de cerimonious distance betwixt de lady dat gibs de order and de indervidual what obeys be strictually obserbed. — Am dat de troof, Miss Jessie?

JESSIE. The major-domo is correct, kidminster: you are about to receive your first instructions in the art of waiting on a lady.

CHARLIE. Waiting on an artful lady is more in my line.

JESSIE. Silence, sir, — from an adept in the profesh.

PETE. Dat's me, I'se in debt.

CHARLIE. Well, fire away, old corkscrew.

JESSIE. You are to imitate him in every particular.

CHARLIE. All right, my lady. (*Going* R.)

JESSIE. Where are you going?

CHARLIE. To black up, of course. "Imitate him in every particular," you said.

JESSIE. No matter about that: I'm color-blind.

PETE (*pompously*). Now, den, in de fust place, fustly, clar de table.

CHARLIE (*imitating*), Clar de table. (*Sweeps books off table with his hand on to* PETE'S *foot*.)

PETE (*seizing one foot, and hopping across stage on the other*). Oh, golly! smash, smash, smash! wha'—wha' d'ye call dat?

CHARLIE (*picking up book, and reading title on back*). "Bunyan's Works."

PETE. Jes' work all de bunions out dat ar foot. Remobe de clof.

CHARLIE. Dar she be. (*Snatches cloth, and throws it over* PETE'S *head*.)

PETE. Dat's 'nuf, dat's 'nuf.

CHARLIE. De table am cleared. What next, Major Dummy?

PETE. Take de lady's order, an' clar yerself.

CHARLIE (*rubbing his hands, and bowing extravagantly*). Now, madam, what is it? fish, flesh, or fowl, baked, fried or broiled: order what you like, it will be sure to be what we are just out of.

JESSIE. Something light, thank you. Paté de foie gras, with chow-chow, tutti fruiti with madeira jelly, charlotte-russe, Italian cream, and—and—

CHARLIE. A physician?

JESSIE. Sir?

CHARLIE. Well, we'll have him a little later by way of dessert, but you'll want him all the same.

PETE. Can you remember the lady's order, sar?

CHARLIE. Yas sar. Patti de fruitti, chow-chow madeira, jelly russe, charlotte froi gras, and—and— Have it on de table fus' class, in a jiff. (*Exit* R.)

JESSIE. Ha, ha, ha! he'll be sure to make a mess of it.

PETE (*crosses to* L. *while speaking*). 'Spec' he will, Miss Jessie. Shouldn't wonder if he fotched it all in a tureen: have chow-chow and chowder den. Why, dem ar stujent fellers, jes' look at it, look at it! Dar edication in dem ar observatories begins wid de free R's, readin', 'ritin', an' 'rithmetic; an' dey think dar edication as waiters begins wid de free S's, fur its nuffin' but smash, smash, smash, and dar dey sticks. Only been hyar free days, an' dat ar pore ole landlord jes' telumgraf for a crate ob crockery: ef dey stop free days more, dey'll broke de whole concern, and dribe the hotel into insolbency an' de landlord into de howling wilderness. Dat's jes' what dey'll do.

JESSIE. Ha, ha, ha! but you shall teach *our* stujent to do better. Here he comes.

(*Enter* R., CHARLIE, *with dishes on waiter in a tablecloth; stumbles at door, and nearly falls upon table, where he deposits his burden.*)

CHARLIE (*turning cloth down round the table, and disclosing food and dishes*). Any thing else, my lady?

PETE (L. *of table*). Let me see: hm, hm! berry nice, berry nice for you. Now place a chair fur de lady.

CHARLIE (*places chair behind table*). Jes' so, major.

JESSIE (*sitting*). Thank you: here is every thing a devouring passion could wish. (CHARLIE *starts for door* R.)

PETE (*snaps fingers*). Hyar! whar you gwine?

CHARLIE. The lady says she has every thing —

PETE. Take yer place behind de lady's cheer: put yer left hand on yer hip, yer right on de back ob de cheer, (CHARLIE *obeys*), and look hopeful.

CHARLIE. Hopeful of what?

PETE. Dat you'll git a quarter.

JESSIE (*looks up at* CHARLIE). A little pepper, please.

CHARLIE (*comes to* R. *of table, hands pepper*). Here you are.

JESSIE. Shake it, please.

CHARLIE. Certainly. (*Holds up the pepper-box without inverting it, and shakes it violently.*)

PETE. Hyar! stop dat! (*Snatches the box.*) On to de patti. Like dis (*shakes it gently on plate*). See?

CHARLIE. See? of course I do. (*Snatches up another box, and shakes pepper on plate.*)

PETE. Hyar, dat ar kyan, stop! stop!

CHARLIE. Of course. Cayenne is healthy (*shakes*), cayenne is good for all kinds of food (*shakes violently over the table*).

PETE. You'll ruin de hole. Gib me dat!

CHARLIE. Certainly. (*Shakes pepper in his face.*) All you want. 'Twill make you smart, old man.

PETE. Smart? (*Sneezes*) Ah chow!

CHARLIE. The chow-chow shall have some (*shakes*).

JESSIE. Oh, stop! You'll choke — (*sneezes*) ah chee!

CHARLIE (*sneezes*). Ah choo!

PETE. Don't you know better dan to — (*sneezes*) ah chow!

CHARLIE. You began to — (*sneezes*) ah choo!

PETE. Bress my — (*sneezes*) ah chow!

CHARLIE. Hang that — Ah —ah —

JESSIE (*sneezes*). Ah chee!

PETE (*sneezes*). Ah chow!

CHARLIE (*sneezes*). Ah choo!

JESSIE (*rises*). Take away the — (*sneezes*) ah chee! My eyes are — (*sneezes*) ah chee! Ah chee! Ah chee! (*Runs off* L.)

CHARLIE. I've made it hot — (*sneezes*) ah choo!

PETE. Hot? (*Sneezes*) Ah chow! Take off dem — (*sneezes*) ah chow!

CHARLIE. Take them yourself. (*Goes* R.) I think, for a lively waiter, I'm not to be — (*sneezes*) ah choo! (*Exit* R.)

PETE. If dis am de fust lesson — (*sneezes*) ah chow! (*takes things from table*) den no more major-domo fur dis chile. (*Sneezes*) Ah chow! Jes' starts de wool ebery time — (*sneezes*) ah chow! (*At door, sneezes*) Ah chow! (*Tumbles off* R., *smash outside*.)

(*Enter* MARTIN, C.)

MARTIN. That fellow Richard Bell troubles me. His sudden appearance here, his recognition of me, his agitation at the sight of Marion, will work mischief, should Poole suspect any thing wrong. Fortunately, he is too well pleased with his acceptance by Marion, to give a thought to aught else; and a speedy marriage will suit him, and make me secure. (*Enter* POOLE, R.) Ah! how speeds your wooing?

POOLE. Not as I should like. True, I have her promise, but her cool treatment of her accepted suitor is something I did not bargain for. Egad! one would imagine from her behavior that I was the rejected, and Jerome the accepted. She's all smiles for him, and calm, cold, statuesque beauty for me.

MARTIN. Coquetry, my boy. Soon she will be all your own.

POOLE. The quicker the better. That fellow, in the face of her refusal, told me he would win her yet; and if Pa

Moore doesn't take a hand in the game, he's likely to keep his word.

MARTIN. What would you have me do?

POOLE. Take her away from this place, — away from Jerome.

(*Enter* MAJOR, R., *staggering, singing.*)

> "Thrust to luck, thrust to luck,
> Stare fate in the face;
> Your heart must be asey
> If it's in the right place."

(*Hic*) That's thrue for ye's, me bys; an' it's a loight heart makes a heavy head the nixt mornin' (*hic*), as I've oftin towld you, Martin, me by.

MARTIN. Major, you've been drinking.

MAJOR. Who towld ye (*hic*), me by? Sure I wouldn't be afther disgracin' the rael owld stingo from St. Domingo, by jingo! by betrayin' (*hic*) it. Sure, I've been praparing meself for what the powets call (*hic*) balmy slape, by the latist medical dishcovery that it's onwise to slape wid an impty shtomach (*hic*), — by getting full, me bys. (*Yawns.*) Bedad! the balm is working. (*Staggers to lounge.*)

MARTIN. Go to bed, old man: that's the place for you.

MAJOR (*stretching himself on lounge*). Faith, how would I know the resate put me to slape, onliss I kipt awake to watch it? (*Yawns.*) Me por owld mother used to say (*drowsily*) Patsey, me by — (*snores*).

MARTIN. Fitz, what will you take? (MAJOR *snores.*) When that invitation won't rouse him, he's off sure; no fear of his disturbing us. Poole, you are right: Marion must be removed from here at once. Fortunately, my sister has gone to our house in town: I will send her there.

POOLE. On what pretext?

MARTIN. Mrs. Morris must be taken ill, and Marion sent for. Is there a train up to-night?

POOLE. No: the last went an hour ago.

MARTIN (*aside*). Bah! that man might drop in at any moment. (*Aloud.*) It's a fine moonlight night, the wind is right: you could take a boat, and sail up.

POOLE. The very thing I would like!

MARTIN. All right. You look up a boat at once. (POOLE *goes up,* MARTIN *to* R.) In fifteen minutes I will receive a telegram from my sister requesting Marion to come at once. (*Aside.*) It's a clumsy piece of business; but it will give me time, and get Poole out of the way. (*Exit* R.)

POOLE (*at* C. *door*). He will trust his daughter in my charge. Ah, hopeful Jerome! I shall score one point against you. (*Exit* C.)

MAJOR (*jumping up*). Bedad! with mischief brewin' it's toime I was convaliscin'. There's no train op the night, but I'm moightily misthaken if there's not one down. Where's the paper? (*Picks it up from floor and looks over it.*) Yis, all roight (*about to drop paper; looks at it again, reads*). Phat's that! the owld reward again? Foive hundred dollars reward — Nathan Roberts — Californian, with his — phat's that? his daughter, ah, ha! that's new. Perkins and Jerome. Jerome, that's — By the howly poker! Twinty years ago! Bedad! Major, me by, there's a big reward winkin' at you, moind that. But foirst I must tiligraf Mrs. —

(*Enter* POOLE, C.)

POOLE. What's this, Major? had your nap out?

MAJOR (*feigning drunk*). Poole, me by, I was jist afther (*hic*) looking for me nightcap.

POOLE. You'll get it at the bar. Where can I find a boatman?

MAJOR. At the helum, me by (*hic*), poipin' his oye at the angry clouds, or eyin' his poipe at the want of tobacyer (*hic*).

POOLE. Pshaw! I want a boat and a boatman at once. Find one for me, and I'll stand a bottle.

MAJOR (*aside*). I'm wastin' toime. (*Aloud.*) Lave it to me, me by, I'll foind it; if there's a boat afloat, I'll foind it if I have to go to the botthom of the say for it. (*Exit* R., *singing.*)

"A boat, a boat, to cross the firry,
For we are goin' to be mirry."

POOLE (*goes up*). He has the happy faculty of blundering into luck. I'll trust him.

MARION (*outside*). Ah, Mr. Jerome, your arguments are profound (*enters* C., *accompanied by* JEROME), but not convincing.

JEROME. You will still listen to me?

POOLE (*aside*). Again together! (*Aloud.*) May I have a word with you, Marion?

MARION (*coldly*). Not just now. I am engaged.

POOLE. To me, yes.

MARION. Is it necessary to continually remind me of that unpleasant fact?

POOLE. Since you continually forget it, yes.

MARION. Forget it? You need not fear that. I am pledged to you, and in due time shall become your wife. You will find me an obedient one; but until that time I am my own mistress.

POOLE. As you will always be. (*Bows.*) Excuse me for interrupting you. (*Goes up in door.*) Cool, and before him too! (*Exit* C.)

JEROME. Marion, have you thought what your life would be with that man?

MARION. Certainly, the common lot of those who slave under a curse. That man's ambition is pleasure. He will tire of me in a month, and then seek the society of others, boon companions in revelry. As time speeds, I shall find myself a burden to him. As he grows careless, I shall become anxious, fearful; by day cower under his fierce humors; by night lie awake far into the still morning with sharpened ear listening for the first faint echo of a stumbling footfall, or awake from fitful slumber to see a demon standing over me with murder in his fierce and bloodshot eye. Oh, Heaven help me! I have seen it all.

JEROME. Marion, you have conjured up visions too hideous to be realized. You will never marry that man.

MARION. Oh! but I will, and bravely too.

JEROME. Because you are driven to it by a father's command?

MARION. Children should obey —

JEROME. You are not a child. As you just now said, you are your own mistress. Assert your independence, and marry the man you love.

MARION. I shall obey my father.

JEROME. Then, if your father should bid you renounce Poole, and marry me?

MARION. I should believe the age of miracles had returned.

JEROME. And welcome it?

MARION. Do not try to entrap me into a confession I have no right to make. I have made my choice, wisely or unwisely : I must abide the consequences.

JEROME. You have wisely given your heart to a man who would lay down his life to save you from the consequences of your unwise promise. That man is not content to be defrauded of his rights without a struggle, when a reckless rival seeks to make a woman captive through her fears.

MARION. Ah! you suspect —

JEROME. Your father is in the power of Herbert Poole. To save him you would sacrifice yourself.

MARION. There are other reasons —

JEROME. One other, yes. You fear, that, should you follow the dictates of your heart, fair prospects would be blighted by the disgrace which attaches to the transactions of the gambler and his victim, and so complete the sacrifice; forgetting, in your mistaken zeal for another's welfare, that infamy can only mar by contact, — that, in plucking the precious jewel from its clinging mass of earth and dross, the explorer is enriching himself.

MARION. But if I should tell you there is another reason —

JEROME. Another! Marion, should you tell me there were a thousand, I would assert my claim against them all. Lovers and lawyers are alike unreasonable in suits: only a favorable verdict will silence their appeals. As this happens to be my first case, and as not only my professional reputation but my future happiness are, against greed and fraud, trembling in the scales of justice, I beg the indulgence of the court, — and the courted, — if I respectfully, but firmly, decline being non-suited. I shall interview your father, appeal to his sense of right, convince him that if he is your father —

MARION. If, if! do you, too, doubt he is my father?

JEROME. Marion, what is this?

MARION. The other reason. One who I believe is my friend has told me I am not Martin Moore's daughter. His statement is so strange I scarcely credit it, but yet —

JEROME. You doubt, Marion? I knew your woman's wit would find a way out of the snare. A doubt to a lawyer is like a block of marble to a sculptor: the skilful hand moulds it to any shape that fancy dictates. Out of your doubt I'll shape a wedding-ring.

MARION. Impossible! you can have no help from me, and Major Fitzpatrick is not a man to be trusted.

JEROME. Leave all to me, Marion.

(*Enter* RICHARD BELL, C.)

RICHARD. I beg pardon —

MARION. Come in, Mr. Bell.

RICHARD. I wished to speak to Mr. Jerome, but not to interrupt —

MARION. Do not go: Mr. Jerome is disengaged. Our conference is over. (*Bows, and exit* L.)

RICHARD (*comes down, looking after her*). How like, how strangely like! The same face, the same step, the very tones of her voice!

JEROME. Well, Richard?

RICHARD. The lady, sir, who is she?

JEROME. The daughter of Martin Moore: you know him?

RICHARD. Martin Moore, no. I have heard his name as one of the boarders here, but never met him.

JEROME. Strange, for he is the man whom this morning I stopped in the act of putting a bullet into your then already uncomfortable head. You must know him.

RICHARD. Yes, yes: I remember. We quarrelled years ago, but why did he attempt to kill me?

JEROME. Why did you quarrel with him?

RICHARD. Why do men make beasts of themselves? Why fire their brains with poison till reason is o'erthrown, and maddening desire to rend and kill asserts its sway? Heaven help me, I was mad! (*Sinks into chair* L. *of table, and buries his face in his hands.*)

JEROME (R.). A drunken brawl.

RICHARD. And you tell me that lady is his daughter?

JEROME. His only daughter.

RICHARD. Happy father! So like, so like! O my child, my little daughter!

JEROME. Have you a daughter, Richard?

RICHARD. I had until that night. Had she lived, would have been the living image of that lady.

JEROME (*agitated*). Like her, Marion?

RICHARD. I met this man years ago, in his own saloon;

we drank together many, many times; in maudlin mood we swore eternal friendship, and the next moment sprang at each other's throats like the wild beasts we were. A meddling fool separated us. I seized a heavy tumbler from the bar, and flung it at his head.

JEROME. Well, well!

RICHARD. No more, no more! I have blabbed too much already; but the sight of that lady awoke memories long slumbering, and your honest face invited confidence. Twice you have saved my life, and I thank you, — from my heart I thank you. (*Rising.*) That's what I came for. Now I will go.

JEROME. One moment, Richard. I think I know the reason why Martin Moore attacked you this morning. The tumbler you threw struck him —

RICHARD. No, no! would to heaven it had! It — it — Mr. Jerome, you force me to speak. You won't betray me?

JEROME (*giving his hand*). Richard, look upon me as your friend. True friendship never betrays. You may trust me with your life.

RICHARD. With life or nothing. " Friend," you said : I haven't one in the wide world, but I'll trust you, sir. I haven't tasted liquor since that night twenty years ago.

JEROME. Twenty years ago!

RICHARD. But that night —

JEROME. After you had flung the tumbler.

RICHARD. My little daughter, who was curled up in an arm-chair asleep, awoke at the sound of strife. While my hand was raised, she, the little darling, sprang towards me, crying, " Papa, papa!" The tumbler flew from my hand. I heard her wild scream. I saw my darling's blood deluging the floor. I saw her fall, and fled accursed forevermore. (*Sinks into chair.*)

JEROME. Well?

RICHARD. That's all. My life since then has been that of a boatman on this coast.

JEROME. But what became of the child?

RICHARD. I dared not approach the city again. But I read of the death of a child in a hospital, from injuries, under circumstances that convinced me it was my daughter.

JEROME. Then, you have no proofs?

RICHARD. An accusing conscience is proof enough. I am a murderer.

JEROME. Conscience, avaunt! That won't stand in law. We must have *prima facie* evidence that your child is dead.

RICHARD. Can there be a doubt?

JEROME. A doubt? Yes, a perfect bonanza.

(*Enter* PETE, R.)

PETE. Massa Jerome, dat are crazy feller of yourn got de trimmins, an' jes jumped out of de attic winder, an'—an'—broke his neck short off. Dey want's you down dar, quick. (*Exit* R.)

JEROME. Unlucky mishap! Don't go, Richard, till I return. (*Exit* R.)

RICHARD. Must have proofs? No, no! Should proofs be sought, suspicion will be aroused, and my life endangered. My life! Is it worth the saving? Alone in my little boat, night after night, I have been swept before the fury of the fiercest gales, and prayed that the boiling sea would open and give me rest. In vain! the angry roar of the tempest was stilled, the black storm-clouds parted, and through the rifts star after star appeared. The seething waters sank to rest, and the far-off boom of the breakers fainter and fainter came. Peace to all but the lonely man who craved it most. Welcome the danger; for life is torture, death the only hope of rest.

(*Enter* MARTIN, R.)

MARTIN. You here again?

RICHARD. I am waiting the return of Mr. Jerome, at his request.

MARTIN. Jerome, the lawyer? What have you to do with him?

RICHARD. I have been telling him a part of the story of my life, that part which you know so well.

MARTIN. What have you told him?

RICHARD. All I knew,—of our quarrel twenty years ago, of that mad act which laid an innocent child bleeding at my feet, of my cowardly flight. You must supply the rest, —you who urged me to the act; you, tempter, who in the sight of Heaven are as guilty as I of that foul deed. Tell me, where is my daughter?

MARTIN. Your daughter! Do you, her father, come to me for news of the child you murdered?

RICHARD. Ah! she died, then —

MARTIN. Nothing could save her. She died in my arms at the hospital, to which I conveyed her. Richard Bell, you must fly from this place at once: your life is in danger. I pity you.

RICHARD. Indeed! Is that why you attempted my life this morning?

MARTIN. You committed a dastardly act, the remembrance of which aroused my indignation, and I forgot myself. I would not harm you now; but there are others, who, should they recognize you, would shoot you at sight. Go, go! you are compromising me by your presence here. Were it known that I knew your secret, I should be obliged to answer to the law for concealing a murderer.

RICHARD. I will go. I will compromise no honorable man. I'll go, but tell me first where rests the body of my little darling.

MARTIN (*confused*). Where rests —

RICHARD. Yes: I should like to know where she lies, that sometime I might kneel beside the grave of my lost darling. Heaven knows I loved her, and she knows now that I never meant to harm her. I should like to plant a few flowers above her head, a few mountain daisies she was so fond of, and water them with my tears, even the tears of a murderer. Where did you say?

MARTIN. At Greenwood, in my lot, you will find a little grave, and on the headstone the name —

RICHARD. "Bell," my pet name for her. Is it there?

MARTIN. Yes, yes. You can easily find it. Now go: every moment is full of danger to you.

RICHARD. I care not.

MARTIN. And me?

RICHARD. I will go. Bell, little Bell, we should have been so happy together! and now — Well we shall soon meet. (*Staggers up* C.) My darling — lost — little Bell! (*Exit* C.)

MARTIN. What have I done? Sent him to the grave of my own little girl! He will read the name there. Strange chance that it should be that of his child! Am I in such a strait that I can use that sacred spot to serve my selfish ends? 'Tis sacrilege. I'll call him back, and disclose all. No, no! I have gone too far, I will not falter now. (*Exit* R.)

(Enter CHARLIE, C., *dress as in Act I.; travelling-bag in his hand.)*

CHARLIE.   Fired at last!   After twelve hours' service in the tray and napkin brigade, I have been informed by mine host in the gentlest manner possible for a man whose heart seems broken, — with other things, — that my services were no longer required, and I must either buy him out or get out.   In fact, he gave me particular Jessie; and I shied off to escape a torrent of reproaches, and a shower of blows, which the swift whirling of a long and heavy poker told me would likely be the next proceeding in my direction.   Ah! here comes my tormentor: more "particular Jessie" in prospect.

(Enter JESSIE, L.)

JESSIE.   Hallo, Charlie, I mean kidminster: where are you going?

CHARLIE.   "My pretty maid," — I have been threatened with a sudden attack of an old complaint, which is generally accompanied by a disorganized vision, in which peculiar astronomic appearances are observable, feverish symptoms, remarkable discolorations about the eyes, and a swelling head.   I have taken advice, and purpose following it by "skipping by the light of the moon."

JESSIE.   What! going to leave us?

CHARLIE.   Yes, I feel I must go: he said I must.

JESSIE.   He? Who?

CHARLIE.   The doctor.

JESSIE.   Nonsense! you can be dosed here as well as at home.

CHARLIE.   I don't like the treatment: I'm a *homeo*pathist.

JESSIE.   Have you thrown up your situation?

CHARLIE.   I have.   I hated to do it; for I was becoming very much attached to that dining-hall, and a waiter's life, — so happy I was learning to sing at my labors the old familiar airs, "Wait a little longer," "Waiting at the gate, love," and "Wait till the clouds roll by."

> "I love it, I love it, and who shall dare
>   To chide me for loving to wait in there?"

JESSIE.   Charlie, you have been discharged: that is why you are going off.

CHARLIE. Discharged! nonsense! You should have seen that gray-haired landlord with a poker in his eye, — ah! a tear in his eye, — entreating me to stay —

JESSIE. No longer. Oh, you gay deceiver! Don't I know all your shortcomings, your downsittings and your uprisings? Haven't the boys told me what a slippery fellow you are? You can't deceive me: you've been fired —

CHARLIE. In the furnace of adversity, and come out an imperfect brick. I know it, Jessie: I was not born "to labor and to wait."

JESSIE. Ha, ha, ha! What fun for the boys!

CHARLIE. Hang the boys! I'm going up to town.

JESSIE. No, you're not: you are going to take me out for a stroll on the beach.

CHARLIE. Oh! may I, Jessie?

JESSIE. Yes, and we'll talk over your future prospects.

CHARLIE. *Our* future, Jessie; and you will name the happy day when I shall cease to be —

JESSIE. A waiter. Ha, ha, ha!

CHARLIE. Now, Jessie.

JESSIE. "There's a good time coming, wait a little longer," ha, ha, ha!

CHARLIE. More fun for the boys. (*Exeunt* C., *arm in arm.*)

(*Enter* R., MARTIN.)

MARTIN. Here's the telegram. If Poole does his part, we are safe. (*Enter* MARION, L.) Marion, here is a telegram from your aunt (*gives telegram*).

MARION. My aunt! (*Reads*) "Mrs. Morris seriously ill: send Marion at once. Dr. Jordan." I must go. Is there a train to-night, father?

MARTIN. No; but I have made arrangements to go by boat. Get ready at once.

MARION. But Jessie, does she go too?

MARTIN. She would only be in the way. Hasten your preparations, we have no time to lose.

MARION. I will be ready in a moment.

(*Enter* POOLE, C.)

·MARTIN. Well, have you secured a boat?

POOLE. Yes, and a safe pilot.

MARTIN. Marion, Mr. Poole will attend you.

POOLE. And see you safely to your destination.

MARION. Mr. Poole! I decline his services. I will not trust myself with him. You are my rightful guardian. If you see fit to attend me, well : if not, I go alone.

MARTIN. Girl, what new freak is this? You have given him a right to protect you.

POOLE. And I claim that right. I will not permit you to go alone.

MARION. And I will not permit you to attend me. I can be as resolute as you, sir. I am not yet yours to command.

MARTIN. I command you to go. (*Seizes her hand.*) This is no time for petty whims. Your aunt needs you: even now she may be at death's door.

(*Enter*, C., MAJOR FITZPATRICK, *with* MRS. MORRIS *on his arm.*)

MAJOR. A mishtake, me by: she's comin' *through* the dure.

MARTIN. My sister!

MARION. Auntie!

POOLE. Dished, by Jove!

MRS. M. (*coming down* L. *to* MARION). Why, Marion, I expected to find you sick in bed!

MARION. And I was just going to find you very ill.

MARION (*aside*). Aunt here! It was as I suspected, — a trick.

MRS. M. Marion quite well! O Major! you telegraphed me somebody was dying.

MAJOR (R. C.). Faith, it is myself that's dyin' for your swate society. Shure, that's no loic.

MARTIN (R., *fiercely*). Confound your meddling! You've completely upset my plans. Why did you send for my sister?

MAJOR. Shure, you wouldn't have me lave her out in the cowld, at death's door, whin there's a warm place inside.

POOLE (R.). Major Fitzpatrick, you're a trickster. What is your little game?

MAJOR. Me little game, is it? (*Takes dice from pocket, and holds it up.*) Sixes, me by.

(*Enter* RICHARD, C.)

RICHARD. The boat is ready.

MARTIN. That man again!' Poole, is this your safe pilot?

POOLE. The Major selected him.

MAJOR. The bist on the coast, me by!

MARTIN (*fiercely, to* MAJOR). Blunderer!

MAJOR. One of the misfortunes of ganius, me by.

MARTIN (*goes up* L.C., *to* RICHARD). You are not wanted (*enter* JEROME, R.), except it be by the officers of justice, Richard Bell.

MAJOR. Aisy, me by, you're at say. Richard's not himself at all at all: he's Nathan Roberts.

JEROME (*aside*). Ah, my missing man!

RICHARD. Run to earth at last!

MARTIN. I have warned you once; I have warned you twice; for the third and last time, if you are seen here again, I will denounce you.

RICHARD. Do your worst. I am reckless. I defy you!

MARTIN. You shall answer to the law for a foul and bloody crime.

JEROME (*stepping up, and grasping* RICHARD'S *hand*). He shall meet his accuser, and I will defend him.

(*Picture :* RICHARD *and* JEROME *clasping hands* C., MARTIN L. C., MAJOR R. C., POOLE R., MARION *and* MRS. MORRIS L.; *all looking at* RICHARD *and* JEROME.)

ACT III. *Scene same as in Act I.* JESSIE *on lounge, reading a book.* CHARLIE *seated* L. *of table.*

CHARLIE (*solus*). What an unmitigated nuisance to himself a fellow becomes when he's in love! At the outset, he has inoculated his system with a disease to which fever and ague are no great shakes. If he indulges in rosy dreams, the horrid nightmare of uncertainty wakes him with a cold sweat. He trembles with delight at a smile, he shivers with fear at a frown. He is a chameleon, forever changing his hues; red with joy, pale with fear, green with jealousy, and blue when left out in the cold. That is the sort of fellow I am: tossed to and fro like a rubber ball in the hands of that wilful beauty there, only too thankful if she does not end her game by giving me the grand bounce. By the express command of her high-and-mightiness, I was not to open my lips for thirty minutes. (*Looks at watch.*) Thank Heaven! time's up. (*Softly.*) Jessie! (*Pause.*) Jessie! (*Loud.*) Miss Morris!

JESSIE (*starting*). Good gracious! How you startled me! Well?

CHARLIE. Time's up.

JESSIE. Oh, I'm so sorry!

CHARLIE. Sorry! Pray, may I inquire what remarkable work is so entrancingly interesting that even the calls of affection are disregarded?

JESSIE. Why, it's perfectly lovely, awfully utter, too all but —

CHARLIE. Ah! philosophical, Concord school, and all that?

JESSIE. No: 'tis a romance of the West, — "Carl the Cowboy." Oh, such a hero!

CHARLIE (*aside*). Great Scott! she's unearthed another hero. I tremble. (*Aloud.*) Well, who's "Cowl the Carboy?"

JESSIE. Carl the Cowboy, I said, sir! A modern knight of the glorious West, the free-born child of the prairie, the fearless rider, the unerring marksman, the champion of the lasso, the rescuer of unprotected females, the — the —

CHARLIE. For further particulars, see the " New-York Rustler."

JESSIE. Oh, I just dote on that Carl! He is the realization of my dreams of a perfect hero. If I could only look at such a man! O Charlie! there's a pattern for you: become like him, and I should adore you.

CHARLIE. Now, Jessie, pause. Much as I hanker for your adoration, there's a limit to human endurance; and mine stops just on the edge of the boundless prairie. I'm not going to set my foot on it: you are going too far.

JESSIE. Won't you, for my sake, become a cowboy, Charlie?

CHARLIE. Not even a calfboy. A pretty hero you've dug up this time! a red-shirted, long-booted, loud-swearing, tobacco-chewing, half-horse, half-buffalo, cattle-driver. Bah!

JESSIE. Don't you abuse my hero. I have set him on a pedestal in my heart of hearts.

CHARLIE. Well, shut him up there: if he should break out, the house couldn't hold him.

JESSIE. And you won't go West to oblige me?

CHARLIE. To oblige neither you nor Horace Greeley.

JESSIE. As a test of affection, Charlie?

CHARLIE. Those peculiar phases of love's delirium have become monotonous. I am surfeited with narrow escapes and thrilling situations. Something in the pastoral line might tempt me, but not your friend, or rather fiend, the cowboy.

JESSIE. Then, you decline my request?

CHARLIE. With thanks.

JESSIE. Very well, sir! I know where to look for a man who *will* become the hero I desire.

CHARLIE. He has my warmest wishes for his success as a cowboy.

JESSIE. Either of your college boys would be glad of the opportunity.

CHARLIE. Try them. It's been nothing but fun for the boys; now let them try to please you, and 'twill be fun for me.

JESSIE. Oh, you cruel, heartless — I'll never speak to you again, long as I live! Never! (*Stamps her foot, and exit* L.)

CHARLIE. Never! never! Should she stick to that, I shall lose her. For the first time I have dared to rebel, and I'm frightened. I'll call her back, humbly beg her pardon, and — and.— No, no! That infernal cowboy stands in the way, and I can't swallow him. I'll give her up, and go back to town. (*Turns up stage.*)

(*Enter* JEROME, R.)

JEROME.• Whither bound, Charlie?

CHARLIE. Home. The sea air does not agree with me.

JEROME. But Jessie does?

CHARLIE. Jessie be — Look here, old fellow, it's all up. The pretty but pouty Miss Jessie has found me a new field for missionary labor in the Far West: she wants me to become a cowboy. I kicked, and she stampeded. My dream of love is over.

JEROME. Ah! but you should humor her: if she desires it, be a cowboy.

CHARLIE. Now you're at it. Suppose Miss Moore should request the same favor of you?

JEROME. I should comply at once, and take the first favorable opportunity to appear before her in the dress and with the manners of one of those paper heroes, and thus convince her that the boasted heroism of these prairie plodders is the product of imagination, not of reality.

CHARLIE. I see: a masquerade.

JEROME. An idea which you will do well to adopt. Fortunately I can assist you. I have in my trunk a complete outfit for this character, in which I once masqueraded, and which I thought might be of like use at the festivities here: it is at your service. Go to my room; equip yourself. I will talk with Jessie, and in due season introduce you as a friend from the West. You can manage the rest.

CHARLIE. I can try (*giving hand*). Clifton, you're a brick. I was just ready to crawl through a very small hole on my knees, but this lets me out whooping. Ah, ha! my lady, the free-born child of the prairie, the fearless rider, the unerring marksman, the champion of the lasso, is on the trail.

JEROME. Hush! Here she is.

CHARLIE. I'm off: it's my test now. (*Exit* R.)

(*Enter* JESSIE, L.)

JESSIE. Where's Charlie?

JEROME. He has just left me. He's to take the next train to town.

JESSIE. To town? Without seeing me?

JEROME. Poor fellow! he seems almost broken-hearted I hope you have not been trifling with him.

JESSIE. Trifling with him! Do you call it trifling to ask a man to be a hero?

JEROME. Certainly not.

JESSIE. That's all I asked of him, — just to go West a little way, and be a little bit of a cowboyish hero. Cowboys are heroes, aren't they?

JEROME. There are many noble specimens of sturdy manhood among the rough herdsmen of the West. By the way, we have one here, an old friend of mine, Carlos Corbus.

JESSIE. I should like to meet him.

JEROME. You shall. He tells me he has come East to seek a wife; and now that this little affair of yours and Charlie's is off —

JESSIE. But it isn't: Charlie is off, but I — and the little affair — Run and call him back, will you, please?

JEROME. Too late. He said he must run for the train. Wait until you have seen my friend.

JESSIE. I don't want to see your friend: I want my Charlie. I've driven him off. (*Takes up book from sofa.*) Carl the cowboy (*throws book up stage*), I hate him. (*Exit* L.)

JEROME. Ah, ha! our little maid is getting anxious. (*Enter* MAJOR, C.)

MAJOR. Is it there ye are, me by? Shure, it's in a hape of throuble I am intirely; and if your lagal lore could accommodate me wid a bit of advice, I'd be obleeged to ye.

JEROME. My legal lore is at your service, Major. State your trouble.

MAJOR. Shure, it's all along of the Widdy Morris.

JEROME. Mrs. Morris? Is she troubling you? Have you offended her?

MAJOR. There's no such good luck. She's the offinsive parthy. She's jist bubbling over wid love, and rattling it down on me hid loike a thousand of brick.

JEROME. With love? Major, you must be mistaken.

MAJOR. Don't you belave it, me by. The widdy's no gosling. Whin she sets her oye on a man, she manes business, and wid the foire in that oye she jist frazes to him. Three toimes she swept the mathrimonial board wid her winning hand, an' I'm on deck for the fourth.

JEROME. You must have given her encouragement.

MAJOR. Not the wink of an oye. 'Tis the misfortune of innocince to be misundersthood. It's the woires did it, me by. In the interests of pace and justice I tillegraphed her: "Come down, me darling: somebody's dyin'." Whin she came I mit her at the dapo as a gintleman should, and escorted her to the house as a gintleman should. Since that toime she has me in her oye intirely. If I walk, she follows me; if I sit down, she snuggles op to me loike a chicken onder its mother's wing. The last of the Fitzpatricks is in danger, me by.

JEROME. About that escort from the depot, Major: was any thing said?

MAJOR. Shure, I thried to make meself agraable. Did iver you hear of an Irishman escorting a lady, an' a foine handsome lady as she is, on a dark road in a moonlight night widout spakin', onless he was a dumb fool?

JEROME. Of course you gave her your arm to lean upon.

MAJOR. Ov coorse. You wouldn't lave her alone to lean by herself, would you? I towld her I would support her, and wished upon me sowl it was me extrame happiness to so support her for the rist of her natural existence: sure, that's no lie.

JEROME. There's where you stumbled.

MAJOR. Don't you belave it. She did, and I jist passed my arm around her waist.

JEROME. Ah!

MAJOR. The betther to kape from stumbling, of course.

JEROME. Certainly. A pretty tight squeeze, Major?

MAJOR. Of course: you wouldn't have a man let a lady shlip?

JEROME. Nor such a chance. Of course she thanked you for your attentions?

MAJOR. She opened her lips to; but I wouldn't have her fale onder obligations, and so I shtopped her.

JEROME. In the usual way?

MAJOR. Of course. Who towld you?

JEROME. Major, I congratulate you. Mrs. Morris is rich, comely, and agreeable. Moreover, without *encouragement* she has taken a fancy to you. My advice is, go in and win her: I will see you through.

MAJOR. Say me through! Shure, I could go it blind, had I the moind: if you'll say me out, you'll be doing the friendly act.

JEROME. Then, you do not return the widow's affection?

MAJOR. Oh, bother! that's jist what I'd loike. If I don't want it I must return it, d'ye moind?

JEROME. Then, you must treat her coolly.

MAJOR. Shure, I have, — to ice-crame and the loike; but the more frazin' the food, the warmer she grows.

JEROME. I can do nothing for you. You have given the lady sufficient reason to suppose that you love her.

MAJOR. Begorra, I've done me bist!

JEROME. Should you now retreat, a suit for breach of promise might be the outcome.

MAJOR. Brache of promise! Who tould you I axed her would she be moine?

JEROME. Then, you have popped the question?

MAJOR. Niver a once. I aven axed an invitation to her nixt widding. A standin' invitation — at the roight of the broide.

JEROME. What did she say to that?

MAJOR. That I moight consider the matther settled: I could have the place.

JEROME. You have run your neck into a matrimonial noose. I withdraw from the case.

MAJOR. And lave me hanging? How will I withdraw from the noose?

JEROME. After the wedding I will cut you down with the knife of divorce.

MAJOR. We'll have the divorce foirst: it moight disturb the festivities afther the ceremonies.

JEROME. I believe, Major, you're half in love with the widow.

MAJOR. Shure, that's but half the truth you're belavin'.

JEROME. Then, what is the bit of advice you came to me for?

MAJOR. Sure, it's about the wordin' of a telegram I'll be afther sindin' ye whin I'm in town, consarnin' the foive hunder-dollar reward: would I say as I said to the widdy, "Coome down, me darlin'"?

JEROME. Ha, ha, ha! Major, you have the best of me. You shall have a check in five minutes. Shall I deduct my fee for advice from the amount?

MAJOR. Betther lave your fay where your advice lift me, — hangin' to be cut down afther the weddin'.

(MRS. MORRIS *appears*, C.)

MRS. M. Major, dear.

MAJOR. Yis, my darlin'. (*To* JEROME.) D'ye moind the oye of her?

MRS. M. I'm going down to the shore. Are you very, very busy?

MAJOR. Busy, is it? Faith, your pleasure is the business of my loife.

MRS. M. Then come down, darling.

MAJOR. To be sure I will, me by — angel.

JEROME. Mind your eye, Major. 'Tis rough travelling where you are going, and my advice is to go slow.

MAJOR. Moighty encouraging advice. You may put it in the bill. For shlow toime I'll make the fastest record in the world, me by. — Coomin', my darlin'.

MRS. M. I hope I am not troubling you too much.

MAJOR (*taking her arm*). Faith, ye are, wid fear that you may shlip, so hug tight and go slow, me darlin'. (*Exeunt* C.)

JEROME. With his usual blundering good luck, the Major is on the high road to wealth and happiness.

(*Enter*, L., JESSIE.)

JESSIE. Has Charlie returned, Mr. Jerome?

JEROME. Haven't seen him, Jessie; but I have seen my friend from Texas, and promised him an introduction to you.

CHARLIE (*outside*). No shenanigin', stranger. I eat my meat rare, and don't you forget it.

JEROME. And here he is.

(*Enter*, R., CHARLIE *as the cowboy*.)

CHARLIE. I say, pard, there's no swashability 'bout this ar place. I've sassed five fellers, and not a galoot dared draw his shooter, an' I'm jest spilin' for a fight.

JEROME. Never mind, Carlos, here's metal more attractive. — Miss Morris, my friend Carlos Corbus of Texas.

CARLOS. That's me, pard, Texas born, Texas bred, and bound to die on Texas sile, with my boots on.

JESSIE. Any friend of Mr. Jerome —

CHARLIE. Is yours truly. (*Offers hand.*) Put it there. (JESSIE, *shrinking, places her hand in his.*) Don't be skeered, gal: I'm as gentle as a calf here, but out thar rile me, an' I'm a tearer. That's me.

JEROME. You'll find my friend very entertaining, Jessie. (*Goes up.*)

JESSIE. Don't go, Mr. Jerome.

JEROME. I must: I have business elsewhere, and I want you and Carlos to become better acquainted. (*Exit* C.)

JESSIE (*aside*). I'm afraid of him. (*Sits on lounge.*) -

CHARLIE (*sits on corner of table*). Miss Morris, those eyes of yourn have got the bulge on me: there's fire enough in 'em to set a prairie blazin'. I feel like the treed coon when old Davy Crockett pinted his gun, — "Don't shoot, I'll come down." That's me. (*Goes to lounge, and sits.*)

JESSIE (*jumping up*). But I don't want you to come down. (*Crosses to chair,* R.) I — I don't know what you mean.

CHARLIE (*taking position on table at corner nearest* JESSIE, *as before*). Mean business, that's me. I'm roaring Carlos of the prairie. I'm a dead shot, a boss horseman, and a sure slinger of the lasso. I've a big ranch, a big herd of cattle, and a big heart, all of which is yours truly. Now short, sweet, and to the pint: when will you marry me?

JESSIE. Well, I never!

CHARLIE. Oh, yes, you will. I'll give you a week to get ready. (*Crosses.*) Come (*offers hand*), put it there.

JESSIE (*rises, and crosses to* L.). No, I never heard of such impudence. What do you take me for?

CHARLIE. A bit of a spitfire who's going to take me as her tamer. (*Crosses, and attempts to seize her hand.*)

JESSIE (*crosses to* R.). Never, sir, never! I don't like your style of courtship.

CHARLIE. Perhaps you prefer the Texas style?

JESSIE (*trembling*). The Ter-Ter-Ter-xas style?

CHARLIE (*goes up* C., *and arranges his lasso*). When a Texas cowboy wants a wife, he goes out and lassoes her.

JESSIE (*aside*). Good gracious! I believe he's going to do it.

CHARLIE. After this fash. (*Throws lasso.*)

JESSIE (*running across to* L.). Oh, what will become of me?

CHARLIE. Missed! by the big buffalo! Missed! like any galoot. Ah, ha! spitfire, we'll try another fling.

JESSIE. Oh, please don't! I don't like it.

CHARLIE. You must be mine. I've spotted you, and I'm bound to scoop you. (*Throws lasso.*)

JESSIE (*running and crouching down in front of table*). Oh, help, help! Charlie! Uncle Pete!

CHARLIE. Missed again, by the great grizzly! Must I try the revolver?

JESSIE. Oh, won't somebody come!
(*Enter* PETE, R.)

PETE. Wha — wha — whar's de rumpus? Who call? who call?

CHARLIE. Ah, there's game. * (*Throws lasso over* PETE, *pinioning his arms.*)

PETE. Here, you dar, stop your fool— (*Kicking and struggling.*)

CHARLIE (*goes up to door,* C.). You black scoundrel, how dare you interfere? (*Twitches rope.*)

PETE. You jes stop dat ar'. Can't get my bref. Don't fool, will you?

CHARLIE. You're in the clutches of roaring Carlos. (*Twitches rope.*)

PETE. Quit your roarin', and luf me go.

CHARLIE. You go with me, roaring Carlos (*jerks rope*), the free-born child of the prairies (*jerks*), the fearless rider (*jerks*), the unerring shot (*jerks*), the champion of the lasso (*jerks*), — that's me. (*Exit* C., *dragging* PETE.)

PETE. I's jes' a gone coon (*exit shouting*), luf me go!

JESSIE (*looks around trembling, then rises*). What an escape! A wild man of the West, and I his wife: catch me! I'll take good care to be out of the reach of him and his lasso. Texas courtship, indeed! it may be romantic, but that sort of matrimonial noose is too binding for me. (*Exit* L.)
(*Enter* MARION, C.)

MARION. Is there no escape from this torture? The man I hate pursues me, the man I love avoids me. It is my own foolish act: why should I complain? I thought myself brave in boldly accepting a fate which my better reason told me was fraught with misery. I cannot fulfil my promise. The hope that Clifton Jerome might free me is vain. For three days, though still in the house, he has not approached me. I must believe the worst. Over-confident, he has failed to solve my doubt, and so avoids me. Well, better so: in some weak moment I might have flown to his sheltering arms, and defied my own sense of right and justice. Now, though I may not be his wife, I can honor him above all others. The woman he loves must wed no other. I will fly from this place, hide myself in the city; work, slave, die of want, perhaps: 'tis my only hope of escape.

(*Enter* HERBERT POOLE, C.)

POOLE. Marion, once more I entreat you, make me happy by naming the day when I may call you mine.

MARION. Mr. Poole, once more I beg you to release me from my thoughtless promise. I do not love you.

POOLE. Not now, but you will when you find what a devoted husband I shall be. When you learn to know me better, you will believe in my sincere wish to make you the happiest woman in the wide world, and love me —

MARION. I must decline.

POOLE. I have your promise, your father's consent: I insist.

MARION. Insist?

POOLE. Politely insist. This matter has gone too far. We are known to be engaged by your own free will. I have given no cause for a rupture, and as a matter of business have a legal claim to your hand.

MARION. If you make it a matter of business, I shall have to refer you to my legal adviser.

POOLE. Clifton Jerome, I presume.

MARION. Sir!

POOLE. He is evidently no longer a *rival*, since he has taken particular pains to avoid you of late. (*Enter* JEROME, C.) Clifton Jerome knows Martin Moore's daughter is not for him.

JEROME. If you were speaking of me, you were quite right. (*Bows to* MARION, *and comes down* R.)

MARION (*aside*). 'Twas as I feared. He no longer loves me.

POOLE. You resign all claim to —

JEROME. Martin Moore's daughter? Most assuredly.

POOLE. Then, why are you here?

JEROME. As this lady's legal adviser, and, as such, privileged to approach her at all times.

POOLE. This looks very much like a lawyer's trick. I don't like it.

JEROME. My dear fellow, you are hard to suit. You complained when I professed love for Martin Moore's daughter; and now, when I tell you I withdraw in your favor, you don't like it. If there is any middle course I can pursue to your satisfaction, I shall be most happy to oblige you.

POOLE. And you are this lady's legal adviser?

JEROME. I am. If you doubt it, ask her father.

POOLE. Her father is my friend; is willing, nay anxious, that I should marry his daughter.

JEROME. And the daughter? (*Crosses to* C.)

MARION. Is neither anxious nor willing to marry this man.

JEROME (*aside*). At last! (*Aloud.*) You have her answer.

POOLE. Not to my satisfaction.

JEROME. Of course not. The lady is evidently in earnest, and a graceful recognition of the sublime virtue of resignation on your part would be a manly act.

POOLE. I will not give her up.

JEROME. No: you will still pursue her, bully that you are; you will still force your hateful attentions upon her, still threaten her with ruin, work upon her fears. Do it at your peril! She has spoken, and henceforth between her and you I stand to guard her from the contamination of a gambler and a cheat.

POOLE (*rushing at* JEROME). Do you dare —

JEROME (*folding his arms*). Prove all I have said? Yes, and more. There is a young woman who to her sorrow has accepted your promise as that of an honest man.

POOLE. Ah! (*Starts back.*) Who told you that?

JEROME. One who only waits my motion to tell it to your father.

POOLE. And ruin me.

JEROME. Fulfil that promise, and you are safe.

POOLE. If I refuse?

JEROME. You will be disinherited.

POOLE (*aside*). It's Jennie or nothing. (*Aloud.*) Jerome, you have beaten me. With millions in the balance, love kicks the beam. I cannot fight you and the old man's money.—Miss Moore, you are free. (*Aside.*) I dare not quarrel with him, and I could strangle him. (*Turns at door,* R.) Good-morning. (*Exit* R.)

JEROME (*turns to* MARION). Marion, I congratulate you. One obstacle to your happiness is removed.

MARION. Thanks to you. (*Gives her hand.*)

JEROME (*kisses it*). And I am a step nearer heaven.

MARION. You no longer love Martin Moore's daughter. (*Withdraws hand.*)

JEROME. I still love you.

MARION. And who am I? Can you answer that?

JEROME. In good time, Marion. I am anxiously awaiting one who I hope will fulfil the hope I cherish.

(*Enter* PETE, C.)

PETE. Phew! Nebber had sich a scare in de hole course ob my life.

JEROME. What's the matter, Pete?

PETE. Dat ar' howlin' carless boy jes' yanked me all ober de beach, an' jes' gwin' to souse me in de brine when ole Dick Bell jes' stepped in an' spile de fun for dat ar' Texican lassoonatic.

JEROME. Ah! has Bell returned?

PETE. Yas, indeed. He's comin' arter me. (*Goes to door* R.) If dat ar carless boy wants to play cow wid me agin', I'll butt him into de middle ob nex' week. I ain't de kine. (*Exit* R.)

JEROME. Marion, I want you to overhear my interview with Richard Bell. (*Leads her to door* L.) Step in here; leave the door ajar, and listen.

MARION. More mystery?

JEROME. The clearing of a doubt: you understand?

MARION. No, but I have faith in my legal adviser. (*Exit* L.)

JEROME (*crossing to* R.). And I in an open door and a woman's listening ear. (*Enter* RICHARD BELL, C.) Ah! back again, old friend?

RICHARD (*comes down slowly, takes* JEROME'S *hand*). Yes, back again from a sad pilgrimage. I have been there to that little grave in Greenwood. The sun was shining brightly; flowers were blooming, and filling the air with fragrance; the birds were singing, and her little bed was soft and green. Such perfect peace! I dared not disturb it with a sigh, and my heart was almost bursting with grief. (*Sits L. of table.*)

JEROME.   You found it where you expected?

RICHARD.   Oh, yes! I could not be mistaken.   Her name was on the headstone, — "Little Bell."

JEROME.   You wrote the inscription as I requested?

RICHARD.   Yes.   Here it is. (*Gives paper.*) It was needless: I shall never forget it, never.   Little Bell, my own lost little Bell!

(MARION *appears in doorway* L., *her hand to her forehead as if trying to recall something.*)

JEROME (*reading*).   "Little Bell, born Jan. 5, 1858, died Aug. 5, 1864." (*Aside.*) What's this? died 1864? Ah! Martin Moore, figures won't lie. (*Aloud.*) Tell me, old fellow, about this little girl of yours: where was she born?

RICHARD.   Away up in the mountains of California.   Ah! those were happy days when the little one came.   She brought luck with her.   We struck the gold that we had sought in vain all up and down the banks of our mountain stream.   Happy days!   Far away from temptation I was a man.   There were few bonanzas in those days; I toiled hard with pick and washer, contented if a few ounces reward the labor of a week; happy as I climbed the hill to my little cabin where wife and little Bell awaited my return. I can see it now, the open door, with the good wife standing shading her eyes with her hand, and the little one toddling down to meet her old dad. (MARION *gradually approaches, agitated.*) Every night as I neared home, I gathered a handful of mountain daisies.   The little one was fond of them; and as I came in sight her little hands would be outstretched, and she would cry —

MARION (*throws herself down in front of* RICHARD, *clasping his knees, and looking up into his face*).   Daisies, daisies! for little Bell!

RICHARD (*sinks back in chair, glaring at* MARION).   Ah! the very words, the very voice! what is this?

JEROME.   The voice of nature. (MARTIN MOORE *appears*, C.) Listen to it, Nathan Roberts: the heart of your lost darling pleads for recognition.   Your daughter is before you.

RICHARD (*clasps her in his arms*).   My daughter!

MARTIN (*comes down* L.).   What devil's work is this?

JEROME (*crosses*). You can best answer that.

MARTIN. That man's child is dead, buried in Greenwood.

JEROME. Then the headstone lies. The little Bell buried there died in 1864. Nathan Roberts and his child arrived in New York in 1865. (*Crosses to* R.)

MARTIN (*aside*). Baffled! (*Aloud.*) Marion, I am your father: the man whose arms infold you is a murderer.

MARION (*starts up with a cry*). Ah! a murderer! (*Goes to* L. RICHARD *rises.*)

MARTIN (*seizing her right wrist*). You must away with me at once. This is no place for you.

RICHARD. No, you shall not escape me thus. I am no murderer. The joy of paternity withheld from me for twenty years is restored by the warm embrace of that innocent girl who called me father. Had I been the blackhearted wretch you brand me, my guilty soul would have shrunk in horror from her touch. Let her decide between us.

MARTIN. Answer me this. Did you not, twenty years ago in a place (*enter* PETE, R., *with a waiter and dishes on it*) called The Flowing Bowl—

PETE (*dropping the waiter*). The Flowing Bowl?

JEROME. What do you know of The Flowing Bowl?

PETE. Why, I was waiter down dar. Dat's whar I entered de profesh.

MARTIN. I thought I knew your face.

PETE. Yas, an' I knowed yours all de time; an' Major Fitz too; yas, indeed. Didn't let on becos I was up in de profesh, an' sorter 'shamed ob de ole days.

JEROME. Were you there when a man crazed with liquor assaulted the landlord, and wounded his daughter?

MARTIN. No, he was not present.

PETE. You're mistook, Massa Moore, I was dar. I seed it all.

JEROME. And the child was badly hurt?

PETE. She was awfully skeered. She jes' run to her fader to stop the row, when dat ar' big tumbler come cabim, an'—an' she jes' frowed up her arm so, an' de tumbler strock right on de wrist so (*puts finger across wrist*). She must hab de scar ob it now.

MARION (*wrenches her hand from* MARTIN'S, *steps for-*

ward, holding up her right hand, showing a red scar across wrist). Was it any thing like this, Uncle Pete?

PETE. Dat's it, dat's it. An'—an' dat's de same little girl: how she's growed!

RICHARD. My own dear little girl!

MARION. Father! (*Embrace.*)

PETE. An'—an' dat's de feller what frowed de glass.

MARTIN (*turns to* L.). I can fight no longer.

RICHARD. Pete, you have done me a service I shall never forget. I am poor in pocket—

JEROME. But rich in lands, houses, and stocks. You are a rich man, Nathan Roberts.

RICHARD. Then, you shall lose nothing by your kindly act, Pete.

PETE. Don't mention it: you make me blush. (*Exit* R.)

RICHARD (*to* JEROME). And you who have been my best friend, how can I thank you?

MARION. Leave that to me, father: I've no doubt—

JEROME. Let me speak. Mr. Roberts, having found you a daughter, I am anxious to complete your family circle by providing you with a son. I love your daughter.

RICHARD. As I suspected. I owe you a debt of gratitude I would repay with my heart's blood: that is what you are asking of me. What says my girl?

MARION. I love him, that he truly knows; and life with him would be happiness indeed, but I will not have it thus. Joyful in our re-union, let me not be ungrateful for the past. One who has reared me with a father's care, almost a father's tenderness, stands silent and alone. Remembering the temptations by which he was beset, the ruin that stared him in the face, forgiving all in memory of the kindness in the past, I cannot pass from his life without his benediction. (*To* MARTIN.) Father of the little Bell who lies beneath the turf in Greenwood (*places her hand on his shoulder, and with her right hand seeks his right*), deal with me as you would have dealt with her, had she lived and loved. May I be happy?

MARTIN (*turns*). Heaven bless your union, Marion! You have been a dutiful child. I have wronged you and your father. Reared in corruption and infamy, I am no repentant sinner. I sought to make merchandise of your heart: had I succeeded, I should have rejoiced in my triumph. I failed, miserably failed; but I have still manliness enough to accept defeat without a thought of revenge. From my keeping, go to happier days and better life (*with a struggle*), "little Bell." (*Kisses her hand, exit slowly* L.)

RICHARD. He shall not be forgotten, Bell. Twenty years of tender care blots out all wrongs. We will consider your case, young man. (*Puts his arm around* MARION'S *waist, and leads her up* C.)

JEROME. In your deliberations consider a lifetime of devotion blots out all doubts.

MAJOR (*outside*). Upon my sowl, Mrs. Morris me darlin', I niver had sich a foine shtroll but once before, an' that's now.

(*Enter*, C., *with* MRS. MORRIS *on his arm.*)

MRS. M. Major, I'm afraid I'm doing wrong in consenting to marry you after my sad experience with three husbands.

MAJOR. Niver you moind, me darlin': I'll not imulate their example. I'll not lave you a widdy : on the conthrary, I'll shtop behind, and politely lave you to go first. In that rispict you'll find me the contrariest husband in the world.

(*Enter* JESSIE, L.)

JESSIE. Why, mammie, where have you been ?

MRS. M. On the beach with Major Fitzpatrick, my — my future husband.

JESSIE. Why, mother, you haven't been and gone and done it again ?

MRS. M. Hush, hush, child, no slang! (*They converse together.*)

JEROME. Well, Major, is it settled?

MAJOR. Complately, me by: we put it to vote, and the oye had it. You shall dance at me widdin', and drink our health in the flowing bowl, me by.

JEROME. You must beware of that, Major. Remember the fate of your predecessors.

MAJOR. Lave me alone for that. Shure, I'll thrick the widdy. She'll not have the satisfaction of seeing me dhrink mesilf down among her buried trisures. I'll shware off, and become a follower of the saint.

JEROME. What saint?

MAJOR. St. John, me by.

JESSIE. But what's to become of me?

MRS. M.   Charlie will take care of you.

JESSIE.   But Charlie's gone.

(*Enter* CHARLIE, R.)

CHARLIE.   Not yet, but I'm off by the next train.

JESSIE (*crossing to* R.).   Off where?

CHARLIE.   To the West. For your sake to become a cowboy.

JESSIE.   No, you're not: I hate cowboys. O Charlie, don't leave me! Mother's going to be married, and I want — I want to —

CHARLIE.   To be married?

JESSIE.   If you please.

CHARLIE.   Glory! come to my arms. (*Hugs her.*) The cowboy did it, after all.

JESSIE.   The cowboy?

CHARLIE.   Yes, howling Carlos of the perairie — that's me.

(*Enter* PETE, R.)

PETE.   Jes' what I fought, stujent agin! Hope I may nebber die if I didn't see pieces ob crockery stickin' to dat ar' carless boy's trouserloons!

JESSIE.   Then, you have been deceiving me, sir.

CHARLIE.   Only as a test of affection, Jessie.

RICHARD (*comes down* C., *leading* MARION *on his* L. *to* JEROME).   My daughter has opened her heart to me. Give me your hand. (*Takes* JEROME'S *right hand.*) With gratitude for all you have done for me, and with faith that you are the man of her choice, I surrender to your keeping my treasure. (*Joins hands.*)   In mutual love and trust be happy.   Once more over the troubled waters of my life the tempest is stilled, the black storm-clouds parted, and through the rifts the stars appear; but with no despairing heart I greet the peaceful rest.   Honor and love, with little Bell reclaimed, gloom vanishes with the night, and joy cometh with the morning.

(*Picture:* RICHARD *with left hand on the clasped hands of* JEROME *and* MARION, C.; MAJOR *and* MRS. M., *arm in arm*, L.; CHARLIE *and* JESSIE, *arm in arm*, R.; PETE, *extreme* R.   *Curtain.*)

No. 6 Reading Club and Handy Speaker.

` Edited by George M. Baker.

Price, cloth, 50 cents ; paper, 15 cents.

CONTENTS.

No. 7 Reading-Club and Handy Speaker.

Edited by GEORGE M. BAKER.

Price, cloth, 50 cents ; paper, 15 cents.

CONTENTS.

Sold by all booksellers and newsdealers, and sent by mail, post-paid, on receipt of price.

LEE & SHEPARD, Publishers, Boston.

You will find both Wit and Sentiment in the 50 Choice Selections in the

No.8 Reading-Club and Handy Speaker.

Edited by GEORGE M. BAKER.

Price, cloth, 50 cents ; paper, 15 cents.

CONTENTS.

Sold by all booksellers and newsdealers, and sent by mail, post-paid, on receipt of price.

LEE & SHEPARD, Publishers, Boston.

Acknowledged the Best.   50 of the Choicest Selections in the

No.9 Reading-Club and Handy Speaker.

Edited by GEORGE M. BAKER.

Price, cloth, 50 cents ; paper, 15 cents.

CONTENTS.

The Spinning-wheel . . . . B. F. Taylor.
The Hero-Woman . . . . George Lippard.
The Song of the North . . . . . . Lizzie Doten.
No Color Line in Heaven . . . . .
Gingerbread . . . . San Francisco Argonaut.
A Night Watch . . . .
The Loves of Lucinda . . . . . . Mark Melville.
The Widow of Nain . . . . N. P. Willis.
The Tomato . . . . Charles F. Adams.
Lookout Mountain, 1863 — Beutelsbach, 1880 Geo. L. Catlin.
The Little Girl's Song . . . . . . Sydney Dobell.
" Papa says so, too " . . . . . . Jennie T. Hazen Lewis.
The Poetry of Iron . . . . Burlington Hawkeye.
Hannah . . . .
An Old Man's Dreams . . . . . . Eliza M. Sherman.
Don Squixet's Ghost . . . . . . Harry Bolingbroke.
The King's Bell . . . . Eben E Rexford.
The Tramp of Shiloh . . . . . . Joaquin Miller.
Johnny on Snakes . . . . . .
Antony to Cleopatra . . . . . . Gen. Wm. H Lytle.
Cleopatra Dying . . . . Thom. S. Collier.
Cheek . . . . Phillips Thompson.
The Right must Win . . . . . . Frederic William Faber.
Make the Best of Everything . . . .
The Dagger Scene from " The Wife " . . J. Sheridan Knowles.
The Calif . . . . Ida T. Thurston.
The Man wich didn't drink Wotter . . .
Mice at Play . . . . Neil Forrest.
Jan Steener's Ride . . . . . . John W. Chadwick.
Setting a Hen . . . .
The Marked Grave . . . . Lillie E. Barr.
A Very Naughty Little Girl's Views of Life
The Dandy Fifth . . . . Frank H. Gassaway.
The Holly Branch . . . . . . " Brownie."
Antoinette . . . . Francis A. Durivage.
Claribel's Prayer . . . . . . Lynde Palmer.
The Marriage of Santa Claus . . . .
A Similar Case . . . .
Selling the Farm . . . . . . Beth Day.
" He and She " . . . . Edwin Arnold.
The Legend of the Organ-builder . . Julia C. R. Dorr.
The One-Legged Goose . . . . .
The Owl Critic . . . . James T. Fields.
Time . . . . Robertson.
The Sleep . . . . Mrs. E. B. Browning.
She would be a Mason . . . . . James C. Laughton.
The Legend of Saint Barbara . . . Mary A. P. Stansbury.
Reviving de Sinners . . . . . .
Awfully Lovely Philosophy . . . .
Life in Death . . . . B. P. Shillaber.

Sold by all booksellers and newsdealers, and sent by mail, post-paid, on receipt of price.

LEE & SHEPARD, Publishers, Boston.

Nº 10 Reading-Club and Handy Speaker.

Edited by GEORGE M. BAKER.

Price, cloth, 50 cents ; paper, 15 cents.

CONTENTS.

LEE & SHEPARD, Publishers, Boston.

No. 11 Reading-Club and Handy Speaker.

Edited by GEORGE M. BAKER.

Price, cloth, 50 cents; paper, 15 cents.

CONTENTS.

No. 12 Reading-Club and Handy Speaker.

Edited by GEORGE M. BAKER.

Price, cloth, 50 cents; paper, 15 cents.

CONTENTS.

No.13 READING-CLUB and HANDY SPEAKER,

Edited by George M. Baker.

Price, cloth, 50 cents ; paper, 15 cents.

CONTENTS.

www.ingramcontent.com/pod-product-compliance
Lightning Source LLC
Chambersburg PA
CBHW030025030726
47499CB00008B/3119